STORIES ROUND THE WORLD

British Library Cataloging in Publication Data

Stories round the world.
I. Federation of Children's Book Groups
808.83 [J]

ISBN 0-340-51260-1
ISBN 0-340-51270-9 pbk

Published by Hodder and Stoughton Children's Books,
a division of Hodder and Stoughton Ltd,
Mill Road, Dunton Green, Sevenoaks, Kent TN13 2YA

Typeset by Litho Link Ltd, Welshpool, Powys, Wales

Printed in Great Britain by Richard Clay Ltd, Bungay, Suffolk

STORIES
ROUND THE
WORLD

Hodder & Stoughton

LONDON SYDNEY AUCKLAND TORONTO

Contents

The Federation of Children's Book Groups, a registered charity, was founded by Anne Wood in 1967 for parents who were interested in knowing more about children's books. Throughout the United Kingdom and other parts of the world, you will find enthusiasts participating as group, professional or individual members.

Each group works independently but with the common aim of opening up the world of books to children of all ages. By organising local book fairs, by story-telling sessions in libraries, schools, children's homes and hospitals and by selling books in all sorts of unlikely places members work to promote delight in stories and in books.

Each year, the Executive committee, which steers the purpose and aims of the Federation, also organises National Tell-a-Story Week during the month of May. Since 1979, it has administered The Children's Book Award, for which children test and choose the best book of the year. The Prize is a silver and oak sculpture and a portfolio of children's comments and artwork.

When the United Nations announced that 1990 was to be International Literacy Year, the Federation initiated the Story Aid project to raise money, mainly through story-related activities, for literacy and educational projects worldwide. 'Stories Round the World' is part of this project.

For further details about the work of the Federation of Children's Book Groups please write (enclosing a stamped addressed envelope) to:
Mrs Marianne Adey, The Old Malt House, South Street, Aldbourne, Marlborough, Wilts SN8 2DW.

Introduction

The story behind this anthology is fascinating. When Hodder and Stoughton asked the Federation of Children's Book Groups if we would like to compile another anthology of stories, our third, to be published in 1990, several ideas seemed to click into place. We had already learned that 1990 was to be International Literacy Year and had begun to make plans for our contribution to the worldwide activities – Story Aid. **Stories Round the World** seemed therefore a natural choice as the theme of our new anthology. In keeping with many Federation activities, including previous anthologies, children were to be involved and were to be the judges.

First we asked everyone in the Federation to suggest favourite stories. We requested stories that had a strong geographical or cultural background. To the list sent in by our members, the coordinators added several more titles so that the balance would include animal, mythical and contemporary stories. A total of 57 short stories was sent to our groups and individual members in sets of ten stories. For three months these sets of stories were tested by the children and the questionnaires were completed. Some were tested by children reading on their own, some by teachers reading to their class, many by parents during family story telling. Over twenty-one and a half thousand children – from Bangkok to Birmingham and from Darwin in Australia to Dysart in Fife – took part in the testing of these short stories. This unique collection reflects their preferences.

By going straight to those for whom the anthology was intended, the selectors set themselves a long and challenging task with thousands of children's replies and comments to consider.

Our aim has been to make a collection for families and teachers to share with children. These fifteen stories are arranged according to age. We have started with those for the youngest children, but there is nothing included that teenagers won't enjoy too.

Stories Round the World is so much more than a title or a collection of stories. Families round the world suggested the stories and shared in their testing. We hope this anthology will help bring our love of storytelling to others, and that through the funds raised from Story Aid it may spread literacy round the world.

Thelma C. M. Simpson,
National Chairman 1988-89

Once There Were No Pandas

Margaret Greaves

Long, long ago in China, when the earth and the stars were young, there were none of the black-and-white bears, that the Chinese call *Xiong mao* and that we call 'pandas'. But deep in the bamboo forests lived bears with fur as white and soft and shining as new-fallen snow. The Chinese called them *Bai xiong* which means 'white bear'.

In a small house at the edge of the forest lived a peasant and his wife and their little daughter, Chien-min.

One very hot day, Chien-min was playing alone at the edge of the forest. The green shadow of the trees looked cool as water, and a patch of yellow buttercups shone invitingly.

'They are only *just* inside the forest,' said the little girl to herself. 'It will take only a minute to pick some.'

She slipped in among the trees. But when she had picked her flowers, she looked around puzzled. There were so many small paths! Which one led back to the village?

As she hesitated, something moved and rustled among the leaves nearby. She saw a delicate head with big ears, a slim body dappled with light and shadow, It was one of the small deer of the forest. Chien-min had startled it, and it bounded away between the trees. She tried to follow, hoping it might lead her home. But almost at once it was out of sight, and Chien-min was completely lost.

She began to be frightened. But then she heard another sound – something whimpering not far away. She ran towards the place, forgetting her fear, wanting only to help.

There, close to a big thorny bush, squatted a very

small white bear cub. Every now and then he shook one of his front paws and licked it, then whimpered again.

'Oh, you poor little one!' Chien-min ran over and knelt beside the little bear. 'Don't cry! I'll help you. Let me see it.'

The little cub seemed to understand. He let her take hold of his paw. Between the pads was a very sharp thorn. Chien-min pinched it between her finger and thumb, and very carefully drew it out. The cub rubbed his head against her hands as she stroked him.

A moment later, a huge white bear came crashing through the trees, growling fiercely. But when she saw that the little girl was only playing with her cub, her anger vanished. She licked his paw, then nuzzled Chien-min as if she too were one of her cubs.

The mother bear was so gentle that the child took courage and put her arms round her neck, stroking the soft fur. 'How beautiful you are!' Chien-min said. 'Oh, if only you could show me the way home.'

At once the great bear ambled forward, grunting to the cub and his new friend to follow. Fearlessly now, Chien-min held on to her thick white coat and very soon found that she was at the edge of the forest again, close to her own home.

From that day on, she often went into the forest. Her parents were happy about it, knowing their daughter was safe under the protection of the great white bear. She met many of the other bears too, and many of their young, but her special friend was always the little cub she had helped. She called him *Niao Niao*, which means 'very soft', because his fur was so fine and beautiful.

The mother bear even showed the little girl her secret home, a den in the hollow of a great tree. Chien-min went there many times, played with the cubs, and learned the ways of the forest. Always the great she-bear led her safely back before nightfall.

One warm spring afternoon, Chien-min was sitting by the hollow tree, watching the cubs at play, when she saw a stealthy movement between the bamboos. A wide, whiskered face. Fierce topaz eyes. Small tufted ears. A glimpse of spotted, silky fur.

Chien-min sprang up, shouting a warning. But she was too late. With bared teeth and lashing tail, the hungry leopard had leaped upon Niao Niao.

Chien-min forgot all her fear in her love for her friend. Snatching up a great stone, she hurled it at the leopard. The savage beast dropped his prey but turned on her, snarling with fury. At the same moment, the she-bear charged through the trees like a thunderbolt.

The leopard backed off, terrified by her anger. But as he turned to run, he struck out at Chien-min with his huge claws, knocking her to the ground.

The bears ran to Chien-min, growling and whining and licking her face, but the little girl never moved. She had saved Niao Niao's life by the loss of her own.

News of her death swept through the forest. From miles away, north, south, east and west, all the white bears gathered to mourn. They wept and whimpered for their lost friend, rubbing their paws in the dust of the earth and wiping the tears from their eyes. As they did so, the wet dust left great black smears across their faces. They beat their paws against their bodies in bitter lamentation, and the wet dust clung to their fur in wide black bands.

But although the bears sorrowed for Chien-min, and her parents and friends mourned her, they were all

comforted to know that she was happy. Guan-yin, the beautiful Goddess of Mercy, would give her a special place in heaven, where her selfless love for her friend would always be rewarded.

And from that day to this, there have been no white bears, *Bai xiong*, anywhere in China. Instead there are the great black-and-white bears, *Xiong mao*, that we call 'pandas', still in mourning for their lost friend, Chien-min.

What the children said:

'*I like the way she wrote it.*'

'*I liked it when the girl pulled a thorn out of the panda's foot.*'

Mighty Mountain and the Three Strong Women

Irene Hedlund
English version by Judith Elkin

Many years ago in a small village in Japan, a huge baby was born. He was so big that everyone called him Baby Mountain.

By the time he was twelve, he was the biggest, strongest boy in the school and the wrestling champion of the whole village. The people in the village were proud of their enormous champion and called him Mighty Mountain.

One warm autumn day, Mighty Mountain decided he must leave the village. He would go to the capital and become a famous wrestler. Every year, the Emperor held a grand wrestling match to find the strongest man in all Japan. Mighty Mountain was sure that he could win.

It was a long walk to the capital and Mighty Mountain strode along, humming to himself. At each step, the ground shook, birds fell from the trees, and animals scurried away in terror.

Mighty Mountain didn't even notice. He was too busy thinking how wonderful he was. Everyone loved him because he was so big and strong. He was quite sure that he was the best-looking wrestler in all Japan, but of course he was far too modest to boast about it.

Just then, Mighty Mountain noticed a girl filling her bucket with water. She was very pretty, with pink cheeks, shining black hair and sparkling eyes.

As the girl climbed on to the footpath in front of him, Mighty Mountain grinned to himself. What fun it would be to tickle her and make her spill the water. Perhaps he could walk home with her and help her to carry the bucket.

Mighty Mountain crept up behind the girl and poked a giant finger in her side. The girl squealed and giggled, but she didn't spill the water. Then, before Mighty Mountain could move away, she trapped his massive hand under her arm.

Mighty Mountain was delighted. Playful as well as pretty, he thought. He tried to pull his hand away, but it wouldn't budge. He pulled harder.

'Let me go,' he laughed. 'You're very strong for a girl, but I don't want to hurt you.'

'Oh, don't worry about that,' giggled the girl, 'I love strong men. Try pulling harder.' She smiled sweetly at him.

But the harder he pulled and tugged, the tighter the girl's grip seemed to get. She began to walk on, dragging the wrestler behind her.

'Please, let me go,' he begged. 'I'm Mighty Mountain, strongest and bravest of all the wrestlers and I'm on my way to take part in the Emperor's Wrestling Match.'

'Oh, you must come and meet Grandma, then. You seem tired. Let me carry you to our house.'

'Certainly not. Just let me go!'

The girl stopped and seemed to look right inside him.

'I'm sure you're a good wrestler,' she said kindly, 'but what will you do when you meet someone who is really strong? You've got three months before the wrestling match. I know because Grandma thought of taking part. If you come home with me now, we could make you into the strongest man in all Japan. Otherwise, you will only spend all your time in bad company and lose what little strength you've got.'

'I don't need help from you, or Grandma, or anyone else,' roared Mighty Mountain, but a tiny shadow of doubt had begun to creep into his mind. He *was* feeling tired and his knees had gone quite weak. If he refused to go with the girl, she might easily break his arm or throw him down the steep mountainside.

He nodded wearily. The girl let him go. He peered down miserably at his red, swollen hand and wondered what he had let himself in for.

They came at last to a small thatched hut high up in the mountains. The girl pointed to two tiny feet in the doorway. Grandma was having her afternoon nap.

Round the corner of the hut came a woman carrying a cow on one shoulder. It was the girl's mother, back from working in the fields. When she caught sight of them, she put the cow down and hurriedly brushed the cowhair off her clothes.

'The poor cow gets sore feet, if I let her walk on the stony paths,' she explained to the astonished Mighty Mountain. 'Who is this nice young man, Kuniko?'

Kuniko told her. The two women walked around the wrestler, looking him up and down. Mighty Mountain giggled nervously and puffed out his chest and arms to show his huge muscles.

'Mm,' said Mother, 'he looks delicate. He needs some proper food.'

Then Kuniko called Grandma. She shouted very loudly because Grandma was a little deaf. The tiny feet started to kick furiously.

'All right, all right, I'm coming!'

A tiny, very wrinkled, toothless old lady shuffled out, leaning heavily on a stick. She stumbled over the roots of the great oak tree in the yard.

'Ow . . . ow . . . ow . . .' she muttered. 'My eyes aren't what they used to be. That's the third time this week I've bumped into that silly old tree.'

She put her thin arms round the trunk and pulled it

straight out of the ground.

'Throw it away, dear,' she said to her daughter, 'I don't think my poor old back could manage it. Mind it doesn't get in anyone's way. You know how clumsy you are.'

Kuniko's mother threw the tree. It flew through the air like a rocket, getting smaller and smaller until it landed on the far mountainside.

Mighty Mountain could stand no more. His face went pale, his eyes glazed over and his massive legs trembled. Suddenly, with a terrific thump, he crumpled to the ground.

Mighty Mountain had fainted.

Grandma noticed him for the first time, as he crashed at her feet. 'Who's this?' she cackled.

Kuniko gently cradled Mighty Mountain in her arms. 'Poor weak man,' she whispered. 'Do you think we could get him ready for the ring in only three months?

Grandma sighed. 'Well, it's not long,' she said, 'and he's a feeble-looking fellow.' She bent down and flung him over her shoulder. Leaning heavily on her stick, she hobbled back into the hut and threw him on the bed.

The next day, the three women set to work.

Very early every morning, Kuniko dragged Mighty Mountain out of bed and made him bathe in the icy stream. Each day, Mother boiled his rice in less and less water, until he could eat food no ordinary man could even chew. Grandma made him work harder and harder and carry heavier and heavier loads.

Every evening, Mighty Mountain practised wrestling with Grandma. Grandma was so old and frail that she couldn't do him too much harm. The exercise might even help her rheumatism.

As the days grew colder and colder and autumn turned to winter, Mighty Mountain got stronger and stronger, almost without noticing. Soon he could pull up trees almost as easily as Grandma could. He could even throw them, but not very far.

Before wrestling practice, Mighty Mountain stamped his foot on the ground. Then the villagers down below looked up at the winter sky and wondered why the thunder was rumbling round the mountains so late in the year.

One evening, Mighty Mountain managed to hold Grandma down on the ground for half a minute.

Grandma's face broke into a thousand wrinkles as she cackled loudly. Kuniko shrieked with excitement and hugged him, almost breaking his ribs. Mother slapped him on the back, making his eyes water.

They all agreed that Mighty Mountain was ready to take part in the Emperor's Wrestling Match.

'We want you to take the cow,' said Mother. 'Sell her and buy yourself a belt of silk, the thickest and heaviest you can find. If you wear it when you greet the Emperor, it will remind you of us and bring you luck.'

Mighty Mountain looked worried. 'I can't take the cow. How will you plough the fields?'

Grandma almost fell over laughing. Kuniko giggled, 'We don't use the cow for work. Mother is five times stronger than any cow. We only keep the cow because she's got such beautiful brown eyes.'

'She's very pretty,' agreed Mother, 'but it's hard work carrying her down to the valley every day to find grass.'

'Then if I earn any money at the Wrestling Match,

20

you shall have it.'

Kuniko blushed, 'Oh, no,' she said, 'we can't take money from a stranger.'

Mighty Mountain grinned at her, bowed low to Grandma and asked if he could marry Kuniko and become one of the family.

Kuniko clapped her hands with joy. Grandma and Mother pretended to give the matter deep and serious consideration, then, with big smiles, they agreed. 'We'll even let you beat us at wrestling sometimes.'

The very next morning, Mighty Mountain tied his hair in a fancy topknot, thanked Mother, threw Grandma up in the air just for fun, and playfully tickled Kuniko.

He ran off down the mountain carrying the cow and waving until he could no longer see the three women.

At the first town he came to, Mighty Mountain sold the cow. She had never worked, so she was good and fat, and fetched a high price. With the money, he bought the thickest and heaviest silk belt he could find. Then he headed towards the capital.

Mighty Mountain hardly noticed the cold as he crunched through the snow in his bare feet. He was too busy thinking of Kuniko and Mother and Grandma.

When he reached the Emperor's Palace, he found that the other wrestlers were already there. They were lazing about, preening themselves, eating large bowls of soft rice, telling fantastic stories and comparing their enormous weights and their huge stomachs. No one took any notice of Mighty Mountain.

In the Palace Yard, the ladies-in-waiting and courtiers waited for the wrestling to begin. They wore layers and layers of clothes, so heavy with gold and embroidery

that they could hardly move. The ladies-in-waiting wore thick white make-up, and the false eyebrows painted high on their foreheads made them look surprised all the time.

The Emperor sat as still as a statue and all alone behind a screen. He was far too aloof and dignified to be seen by ordinary people. The wrestling bored him. He much preferred reading and writing poetry and hoped the wrestling would soon be over.

The first match was between Mighty Mountain and

Balloon Belly, a wrestler who was famous for his gigantic stomach.

With great ceremony, the two wrestlers threw a little salt into the ring to drive away evil spirits. Then they stood, legs apart, facing each other.

Balloon Belly rippled his enormous stomach then raised his foot and stamped the ground with a terrific crash. He glared at Mighty Mountain, as if to say, 'Beat that, weakling!'

Mighty Mountain glared back at Balloon Belly, thought of Grandma and stamped his foot. It sounded like a clap of thunder. The ground shook and Balloon Belly floated out of the ring like a giant green soap bubble. He landed with a thud in front of the Emperor's screen.

'The Earth God is angry,' Balloon Belly stammered, bowing low to the screen, 'I think there's something wrong with the salt. I had better not wrestle again this year.'

Five other wrestlers thought the Earth God might be angry with them, too, and decided not to wrestle.

When the next competitor was ready, Mighty Mountain was careful not to stamp his foot too hard. He just picked his opponent up round the waist and carried him out of the ring.

With a polite bow, Mighty Mountain placed the wrestler in front of the Emperor's screen. Then, one by one, he did exactly the same with all the other wrestlers.

The ladies-in-waiting looked more surprised than ever as they giggled delightedly behind their fans.

The Emperor's shoulders heaved with silent laughter and the plume on his head-dress wobbled in a most undignified manner. He hadn't seen anything so funny for years. He put one royal finger through the screen and waggled it at the wrestlers who were sitting on the ground blubbering. He gave orders for Mighty Mountain to receive all the prize money.

The Emperor congratulated Mighty Mountain. 'But,' he whispered, 'I don't think you had better take part again next year. We don't want to upset these poor babies any more.' He looked at the heap of wrestlers and started giggling again.

Mighty Mountain agreed quite happily. He had decided that he would much rather be a farmer anyway, and he hurried off back to Kuniko.

Kuniko saw him coming from a long way off and ran to meet him. She hugged him carefully, then picked him up and carried him and the heavy bag of money halfway up the mountain. Then she put him down and let him carry her the rest of the way home.

The name of Mighty Mountain was soon forgotten in the capital. But the Emperor never really enjoyed another wrestling match and was always glad when it was over and he could get back to his poetry.

Now and again, the people in the village down below feel the earth shake and hear thunder rumbling round the mountains. But it's only Mighty Mountain and Grandma practising their wrestling.

What the children said:

'It was funny when the wrestlers cried.'

'I liked it when Grandma pulled up the tree.'

The Great White Cat

Amabel Williams-Ellis

Once upon a time, far away in the north of Norway, there was a hunter and he caught a big white bear, alive, in a trap. It was such a fine young bear that he hadn't the heart to kill it, so he thought he would take it to the King of Denmark for a present. So he tamed it, and a very good bear it was.

Now, as bear and man plodded along on their long, long journey to the court of the King of Denmark, they came, just on Christmas Eve, to the Dovrafell. Now the Dovrafell is a bad sort of a place at any time of the year. It's a wild moor, all bog and heather and rock, with hardly a tree for shelter, and it's worst of all in the dark of winter, with the wind roaring and a sky full of snow. However, they hadn't gone far when the hunter thought he saw a light. As he got nearer he saw it must be a candle in a cottage window. Very glad he was to see it, in a wild place like that with the snow coming on.

The hunter knocked at the door and greeted the man of the house politely, and asked if he could get house-room there for his bear and himself.

'You might come and welcome,' said the man, whose name was Halvor. 'But deary me! We can't give anyone house-room, not just now!'

'But it's perishing cold out here in the Dovrafell,' said the hunter.

'So it is,' said Halvor, 'and I'm sorry for you, but we have a bad time in this house at this time of the year. Every Christmas, for years now, such a pack of Trolls come down upon us that we are always forced to flit out of the house ourselves! Deary me! These seven years we haven't had so much as a house over our own heads – not at Christmas – and often not a morsel of food. It's very hard on the poor children, so it is!'

'Oh,' said the hunter, 'if that's all, you can very well let in me and my bear. We're not afraid of Trolls. My bear's a quiet fellow. He can lie under the stove yonder, and I can sleep in that little side-room you have by the kitchen.'

Well, at first, Halvor said it would never do, but it was growing so cold outside, and the hunter begged so hard, that, at last, he and his bear were allowed to stay. So in they came. The bear lay down, and the hunter sat by the stove while the woman of the house began to get ready their Christmas dinner with the three children helping her. The hunter thought it was a queer sight to watch them getting the good things ready, for they had never a smile on their faces though they had managed to get together quite a nice feast, so that the hunter's mouth watered. But neither the good woman nor the children nor Halvor were very cheerful about it all, for, you see, they feared that it would only be the Trolls that would get it after all.

Next day was Christmas Day and, sure enough, no sooner had they all sat down to their Christmas dinner than down came the whole pack of Trolls. Some came down the chimney and some came through the windows. They all shouted and banged about and made such a hullabaloo that, in a fright, Halvor, his wife, and the three children got up from their places without having tasted a bite, and all ran to the woodshed and shut and locked the door. For you see Trolls are ill creatures and, if it had come to a fight, Halvor thought that the whole cottage might have been wrecked and the children hurt.

As for the hunter, he sat still in a corner, and watched to see what would happen. Some of the Trolls were big

and some were little, and all were black and hairy. Some had long tails, and some had no tails at all, and some had noses as long as pokers. They all went on shouting and they put their feet and their tails on the table, threw the food about, and ate and drank, and messed and tasted everything. The little, screaming Trolls were the worst. They pulled each other's tails, fought over the food and even climbed up the curtains and began throwing such things as jars of jam and pickles, *smash*, off the kitchen shelves.

At last, one of these little Trolls caught sight of the great white bear, which all this time lay quiet and good under the stove. The little Troll found a piece of sausage and he stuck it on a fork.

'Pussy! Pussy! Will you have a bit of sausage?' he screamed as he poked the fork hard against the bear's tender black nose. Then he laughed and pulled it away again so that the bear couldn't get the sausage.

Then the great white bear was very angry. Up he rose and, with a growl like thunder, he came out from under the stove and, in a moment, he had chased the whole pack of Trolls out of the house.

So the hunter praised him and patted him and gave him a big bit of sausage to eat in his place under the stove. Then he called Halvor and the family to come out of the woodshed. They were very surprised to find the Trolls gone, and they cleared up the mess while the hunter told them what had happened. Then they all sat

down to eat what was left of their Christmas dinner.

The next day the hunter and the bear thanked Halvor and set out again on their long journey to the court of the King of Denmark.

Next year Halvor was out, just about sunset, in a wood at the edge of the Dovrafell on the afternoon of Christmas Eve. He was busy cutting all the wood they would want for the holiday. When he stopped to rest for a moment, leaning on his axe, he heard a voice that seemed to come from far away on the other side of the wood.

'Halvor! Halvor!' someone was shouting and calling.

'What do you want?' shouted Halvor. 'Here I am.'

'Have you got your big white cat with you still?' called the voice.

'Yes, that I have!' called back Halvor. 'She's lying at home under the stove this moment. What's more, she has got seven kittens now, each bigger and fiercer than she is herself!'

'Then we'll never come to see you again!' bawled out the Troll from the other side of the wood.

What's more he never did, and so, since that time, the Trolls of the Dovrafell have never eaten their Christmas dinner at Halvor's house again.

From *The Enchanted World*

What the children said:

'My favourite bit was, "Have you still got that big white cat?"'

'I liked it when the trolls made a mess.'

Baba Yaga's Daughter

Joan Aiken

There was once a girl called Vasilissa whose mother had died, and whose father married again. The second wife and her two daughters hated Vasilissa because she was so pretty and obedient, because her father loved her best, and, above all, because she was much more skilful than they at making lace, at spinning, and at knitting stockings. So her life was an unhappy one. She had to do all the work of the house, dig the garden, fetch the wood, fill the water-jugs at the village well, and make sure the hearth-stone was hot.

One time the father was away on business, and the stepmother went out to a harvest festival. Before she left, she gave each of the three girls her task for the evening: one was to make lace, one to knit stockings, and Vasilissa was to spin. The mother put out all the fires in the house, and left only one candle burning. But, in secret, she told her daughters to blow the candle out after she had gone. And this they did.

'Now what shall we do?' they said. 'There is no light and our work is not done. We must get a light from the Baba Yaga.'

'I shan't go,' said one of the stepsisters, 'for I can knit in the dark.'

'I shan't go,' said the other stepsister, 'for I can see by the light of my needles.'

Then they both said to Vasilissa, 'You must go and get light from Baba Yaga!' And they turned her out of the house.

Now this Baba Yaga lived in a hut in the forest, and it was said that she ate men up as if they were chickens. So Vasilissa crossed herself and went trembling among the trees. As she felt her way forward, suddenly a knight on horseback galloped past her. He was dressed all in white, and his horse was white, and even his reins; and as he passed it grew light. Vasilissa went a little farther, and a second horseman passed; his horse and saddle were red, and his clothes, and even his reins; when he had passed by, the sun rose. Vasilissa went on. And another horseman passed by who was all in black – his cloak, his horse, and his reins; and night fell again.

Now Vasilissa came to the clearing where Baba Yaga's hut stood: the fence round the hut was made of human bones, and on the fenceposts there were skulls, glaring out of their eye-sockets. And instead of the gate there were feet, instead of bolts there were hands, instead of the lock there was a mouth with sharp teeth. And inside the fence there was a little hut standing on a cock's foot and turning round and round.

Vasilissa went stony cold with fear, for the eyes in all the skulls glared at her, but she walked forward to the hut and called out, 'Hut! Stand still as you should, with your back to the wood.'

At that the hut stood still, and the door opened, and a girl looked out. She was knitting a cloth with gold and silver thread. She greeted Vasilissa with a friendly smile, and exclaimed, 'Oh, my darling, my sister! I am so happy to see you, for here I pass my days all alone. I shall be glad to give you rest and refreshment as long as my mother is not here. But when she comes back, woe to us both, she will eat you up!'

When she heard this Vasilissa was even more frightened, but she said, 'Oh, my sister, let me in I beg you, for I have been sent to fetch a little fire.'

'Well, I will let you in,' said Baba Yaga's daughter, 'and we will think what is best to be done.'

So she let in Vasilissa, set her by the fire, and gave her food. The two girls were very happy together; they sewed, they knitted, they talked, they laughed, and they combed their hair.

Suddenly they heard a terrible noise outside in the forest. The tree branches creaked and the dry leaves rattled, for Baba Yaga was flying back over the trees in her pestle and mortar.

Quick as a flash, Baba Yaga's daughter turned her visitor into a needle, stuck her into the birch-broom, and set her on one side. Baba Yaga came in, and her eyes were gleaming like coals of fire. Her legs were of wood, and her nose was so large that it touched the ceiling. She stretched her jaws beyond measure.

'Tell me, my little one, my daughter, why do I smell human bones?'

'Mother, an old man came past who wanted a drink of water.'

'Why did you not keep him?'

'Mother, he was old and tough; you would not have enjoyed eating him.'

So Baba Yaga lay down and slept. Some hours later, out she went again, flying in her mortar and rowing it with the pestle. For it was day, and the glimmer in the skulls' eyes had dimmed. Then her daughter ran quickly and let Vasilissa out of the birch-broom, and, as before, the two girls sewed, talked, laughed, and combed their hair.

'Tell me, my sister,' said Vasilissa, 'who was the white knight that passed me in the forest?'

'He was the bright day.'

'And who was the horseman all in red?'

'That was the red sun.'

'And who was the horseman all in black?'

'That was the dark night. They are all three my mother's servants.'

Then they heard a terrible whistling and crackling in the forest: Baba Yaga was returning. So her daughter made haste and turned Vasilissa into a needle once more, and stuck her into the birch-broom. Baba Yaga came in, her eyes gleaming like red coals.

'Daughter, my little darling, why does the house smell so of human bones?'

'Two old men passed by and wanted to warm their hands. I tried to make them stay, but they would not.'

'Next time, be sure you make them stay,' said Baba Yaga, and then she lay down and was soon snoring. Next morning, when the glimmer in the skulls' eyes had died away, she went off as before, flying in her mortar and rowing it with the pestle.

Then her daughter made haste and let Vasilissa out of the broom. The girls set to work, sewed, talked, laughed, and combed their hair. But they forgot how time was flying by, and suddenly Baba Yaga stood before them. She seized Vasilissa and cried, 'Daughter, my little one, heat the oven quickly! Make it very hot!'

There was nothing for it. The daughter had to bring in logs of oak and pine, light the stove, and heat up the oven. Then Baba Yaga took her broad wooden shovel and said to Vasilissa, 'Sit on the shovel, dear child!'

Vasilissa did not dare disobey. But she stuck her feet out sideways so that they came against the wall of the hearth.

'Not like that, my little one!'

'How, then, Baba Yaga?' And Vasilissa stuck her feet out on the other side.

'Will you sit still, girl!'

But Vasilissa could not seem to understand how Baba Yaga meant her to sit. At last the witch became angry, and said, 'You are simply wasting time! See, you must sit like this.'

Down she sat on the shovel with her knees up to her chin. The two girls instantly shot her into the oven and shut the door; took their knitting, their comb and brush, and ran out of the hut. As they passed through the gate, Vasilissa took one of the skulls. Then they ran and they ran, but when they looked back, Baba Yaga had managed to burst her way out of the oven, and was running after them, calling out, 'Hoo! Hoo! Hoo!'

So the girls threw the hairbrush behind them, and at once a dense thicket grew up. It took Baba Yaga a long time to struggle through the bushes, but at last she did so and came after them as before, crying, 'Hoo! Hoo! Hoo!'

Then they threw the comb behind them. A thick dark oak forest grew up, and before she could fight her way through it, Baba Yaga had to tear up each tree with her teeth. But at last she came out on the other side and ran after them as before, calling out, 'Hoo! Hoo! Hoo!'

Then they threw the piece of gold-and-silver knitted cloth behind. And it turned to a great marsh. Baba Yaga started to cross it, but she sank, first up to her knees, then to her waist, then to her chin. Then she sank out of sight and was never seen again.

The two girls ran on until they came to Vasilissa's home. There was no light in the window, so Vasilissa knocked and went in.

'There you are!' said her stepsisters. 'Why have you been so long? Ever since you went away we have been unable to get the fire to burn; even if we borrowed a light from the neighbours it went out as soon as we brought it in.'

'Perhaps *your* fire may burn,' said the stepmother.

So Vasilissa brought in the skull. But the fire from its eyes darted out and burned the stepmother and stepsisters to cinders. Then Vasilissa buried the skull in the earth, and called in Baba Yaga's daughter and the two girls lived together happily, sewing, talking, laughing, and combing their hair.

From *The Kingdom under the Sea and Other Stories*

What the children said:

'Oh – good trick.'

'It will haunt you in the night.'

The Pudding Like a Night on the Sea

Ann Cameron

'I'm going to make something special for your mother,' my father said.

My mother was out shopping. My father was in the kitchen looking at the pots and the pans and the jars of this and that.

'What are you going to make?' I said.

'A pudding,' he said.

My father is a big man with wild black hair. When he laughs, the sun laughs in the window-panes. When he thinks, you can almost see his thoughts sitting on all the tables and chairs. When he is angry, me and my little brother Huey shiver to the bottom of our shoes.

'What kind of pudding will you make?' Huey said.

'A wonderful pudding,' my father said. 'It will taste like a whole raft of lemons. It will taste like a night on the sea.'

Then he took down a knife and sliced five lemons in half. He squeezed the first one. Juice squirted in my eye.

'Stand back!' he said, and squeezed again. The seeds flew out on the floor. 'Pick up those seeds, Huey!' he said.

Huey took the broom and swept them up.

My father cracked some eggs and put the yolks in a pan and the whites in a bowl. He rolled up his sleeves and pushed back his hair and beat up the yolks. 'Sugar, Julian!' he said, and I poured in the sugar.

He went on beating. Then he put in lemon juice and cream and set the pan on the stove. The pudding bubbled and he stirred it fast. Cream splashed on the stove.

'Wipe that up, Huey!' he said.

Huey did.

It was hot by the stove. My father loosened his collar and pushed at his sleeves. The stuff in the pan was getting thicker and thicker. He held the beater up high in the air. 'Just right!' he said, and sniffed the smell of the pudding.

He whipped the egg whites and mixed them into the pudding. The pudding looked softer and lighter than air.

'Done!' he said. He washed all the pots, splashing water on the floor, and wiped the counter so fast his hair made circles around his head.

'Perfect!' he said. 'Now I'm going to take a nap. If something important happens, bother me. If nothing important happens, don't bother me. And – the pudding is for your mother. Leave the pudding alone!'

He went to the living room and was asleep in a minute, sitting straight up in his chair.

Huey and I guarded the pudding.

'Oh, it's a wonderful pudding,' Huey said.

'With waves on the top like the ocean,' I said.

'I wonder how it tastes,' Huey said.

'Leave the pudding alone,' I said.

'If I just put my finger in – there – I'll know how it tastes,' Huey said.

And he did it.

'You did it!' I said. 'How does it taste?'

'It tastes like a whole raft of lemons,' he said. 'It tastes like a night on the sea.'

'You've made a hole in the pudding!' I said. 'But since you did it, I'll have a taste.' And it tasted like a whole night of lemons. It tasted like floating at sea.

'It's such a big pudding,' Huey said. 'It can't hurt to have a little more.'

'Since you took more, I'll have more,' I said.

'That was a bigger lick than I took!' Huey said. 'I'm going to have more again.'

'Whoops!' I said.

'You put in your whole hand!' Huey said. 'Look at the pudding you spilled on the floor!'

'I am going to clean it up,' I said. And I took the rag from the sink.

'That's not really clean,' Huey said.

'It's the best I can do,' I said.

'Look at the pudding!' Huey said.

It looked like craters on the moon. 'We have to smooth this over,' I said. 'So it looks the way it did before! Let's get spoons.'

And we evened the top of the pudding with spoons, and while we evened it, we ate some more.

'There isn't much left,' I said.

'We were supposed to leave the pudding alone,' Huey said.

'We'd better get away from here,' I said. We ran into our bedroom and crawled under the bed. After a long time we heard my father's voice.

'Come into the kitchen, dear,' he said. 'I have something for you.'

'Why, what is it?' my mother said, out in the kitchen.

Under the bed, Huey and I pressed ourselves to the wall.

'Look,' said my father, out in the kitchen. 'A wonderful pudding.'

'Where is the pudding?' my mother said.

'WHERE ARE YOU BOYS?' my father said. His voice went through every crack and corner of the house.

We felt like two leaves in a storm.

'WHERE ARE YOU? I SAID!' My father's voice was booming.

Huey whispered to me, 'I'm scared.'

We heard my father walking slowly through the rooms.

'Huey!' he called. 'Julian!'

We could see his feet. He was coming into our room.

He lifted the bedspread. There was his face, and his eyes like black lightning. He grabbed us by the legs and pulled. 'STAND UP!' he said.

We stood.

'What do you have to tell me?' he said.

'We went outside,' Huey said, 'and when we came back, the pudding was gone!'

'Then why were you hiding under the bed?' my father said.

We didn't say anything. We looked at the floor.

'I can tell you one thing,' he said. 'There is going to be some beating here now! There is going to be some whipping!'

The curtains at the window were shaking. Huey was holding my hand.

'Go into the kitchen!' my father said. 'Right now!'

We went into the kitchen.

'Come here, Huey!' my father said.

Huey walked towards him, his hands behind his back.

'See these eggs?' my father said. He cracked them and put the yolks in a pan and set the pan on the counter. He stood a chair by the counter. 'Stand up here,' he said to Huey.

Huey stood on the chair by the counter.

'Now it's time for your beating!' my father said.

Huey started to cry. His tears fell in with the egg yolks.

'Take this!' my father said. My father handed him the egg beater. 'Now beat those eggs,' he said. 'I want this to be a good beating!'

'Oh!' Huey said. He stopped crying. And he beat the egg yolks.

'Now you, Julian, stand here!' my father said.

I stood on a chair by the table.

'I hope you're ready for your whipping!'

I didn't answer. I was afraid to say yes or no.

'Here!' he said, and he set the egg whites in front of me. 'I want these whipped and whipped well!'

'Yes, sir!' I said, and started whipping.

My father watched us. My mother came into the kitchen and watched us.

After a while Huey said, 'This is hard work.'

'That's too bad,' my father said. 'Your beating's not done!' And he added sugar and cream and lemon juice to Huey's pan and put the pan on the stove. And Huey went on beating.

'My arm hurts from whipping,' I said.

'That's too bad,' my father said. 'Your whipping's not done.'

So I whipped and whipped, and Huey beat and beat.

'Hold that beater in the air, Huey!' my father said.

Huey held it in the air.

'See!' my father said. 'A good pudding stays on the beater. It's thick enough now. Your beating's done.' Then he turned to me. 'Let's see those egg whites, Julian!' he said. They were puffed up and fluffy. 'Congratulations, Julian!' he said. 'Your whipping's done.'

He mixed the egg whites into the pudding himself. Then he passed the pudding to my mother.

'A wonderful pudding,' she said. 'Would you like some, boys?'

'No thank you,' we said.

She picked up a spoon. 'Why, this tastes like a whole raft of lemons,' she said. 'This tastes like a night on the sea.'

From *The Julian Stories*

What the children said:

'I wish my daddy would be cross like that.'

'I would eat the rest of the pudding.'

46

The Girl Who Loved Wild Horses

Paul Goble

The people were always moving from place to place following the herds of buffalo. They had many horses to carry the tipis and all their belongings. They trained their fastest horses to hunt the buffalo.

There was a girl in the village who loved horses. She would often get up at daybreak when the birds were singing about the rising sun. She led the horses to drink at the river. She spoke softly and they followed.

People noticed that she understood horses in a special way. She knew which grass they liked best and where to find them shelter from the winter blizzards. If a horse was hurt she looked after it.

Every day when she had helped her mother carry water and collect firewood, she would run off to be with the horses. She stayed with them in the meadows, but was careful never to go beyond sight of home.

One hot day when the sun was overhead she felt sleepy. She spread her blanket and lay down. It was nice to hear the horses eating and moving slowly among the flowers. Soon she fell asleep.

A faint rumble of distant thunder did not waken her. Angry clouds began to roll out across the sky with lightning flashing in the darkness beneath. But the fresh breeze and scent of rain made her sleep soundly.

Suddenly there was a flash of lightning, a crash and rumbling which shook the earth. The girl leapt to her feet in fright. Everything was awake. Horses were rearing up on their hind legs and snorting in terror. She grabbed a horse's mane and jumped on his back.

In an instant, the herd was galloping away like the wind. She called to the horses to stop, but her voice was lost in the thunder. Nothing could stop them. She hugged her horse's neck with her fingers twisted into his mane. She clung on, afraid of falling under the drumming hooves.

The horses galloped faster and faster, pursued by the thunder and lightning. They swept like a brown flood across hills and through valleys. Fear drove them on and on, leaving their familiar grazing grounds far behind.

At last the storm disappeared over the horizon. The tired horses slowed and then stopped and rested. Stars came out and the moon shone over hills the girl had never seen before. She knew they were lost.

Next morning she was wakened by a loud neighing. A beautiful spotted stallion was prancing to and fro in front of her, stamping his hooves and shaking his mane. He was strong and proud and more handsome than any horse she had ever dreamed of. He told her that he was the leader of all the wild horses who roamed the hills. He welcomed her to live with them. She was glad, and all her horses lifted their heads and neighed joyfully, happy to be free with the wild horses.

The people searched everywhere for the girl and the vanished horses. They were nowhere to be found.

But a year later two hunters rode into the hills where the wild horses lived. When they climbed a hill and looked over the top they saw the wild horses led by the beautiful spotted stallion. Beside him rode the girl leading a colt. They called out to her. She waved back, but the stallion quickly drove her away with all his horses.

The hunters galloped home and told what they had seen. The men mounted their fastest horses and set out at once.

It was a long chase. The stallion defended the girl and

the colt. He circled round and round them so that the riders could not get near. They tried to catch him with ropes but he dodged them. He had no fear. His eyes shone like old stars. He snorted and his hooves struck as fast as lightning.

The riders admired his courage. They might never have caught the girl except her horse stumbled and she fell.

She was glad to see her parents and they thought she would be happy to be home again. But they soon saw she was sad and missed the colt and the wild horses.

Each evening as the sun went down people would hear the stallion neighing sadly from the hilltop above the village, calling for her to come back.

The days passed. Her parents knew the girl was lonely. She became ill and the doctors could do nothing to help her. They asked what would make her well again. 'I love to run with the wild horses,' she answered. 'They are my relatives. If you let me go back to them I shall be happy for evermore.'

Her parents loved her and agreed that she should go back to live with the wild horses. They gave her a beautiful dress and the best horse in the village to ride.

The spotted stallion led his wild horses down from the hills. The people gave them fine things to wear: colorful blankets and decorated saddles. They painted designs on their bodies and tied eagle feathers and ribbons in their manes and tails.

In return, the girl gave the colt to her parents. Everyone was joyful.

Once again the girl rode beside the spotted stallion. They were proud and happy together.

But she did not forget her people. Each year she

would come back, and she always brought her parents a colt.

And then one year she did not return and was never seen again. But when hunters next saw the wild horses there galloped beside the mighty stallion a beautiful mare with a mane and tail floating like wispy clouds about her. They said the girl had surely become one of the wild horses at last.

Today we are still glad to remember that we have relatives among the Horse People. And it gives us joy to see the wild horses running free. Our thoughts fly with them.

What the children said:

'I thought it was beautiful.'

'I liked it when the girl came back every year.'

A Navaho's song about his horse:

My horse has a hoof like striped agate;
His fetlock is like a fine eagle-plume;
His legs are like quick lightning.
My horse's body is like an eagle-plumed arrow;
My horse has a tail like a trailing black cloud.
His mane is made of short rainbows.
My horse's ears are made of round corn.
My horse's eyes are made of big stars.
My horse's teeth are made of white shell.
The long rainbow is in his mouth for a bridle,
And with it I guide him.

Black Elk, an Oglala Sioux, had a dream in which he heard a stallion sing a song:

My horses, prancing they are coming.
My horses, neighing they are coming.
Prancing, they are coming.
All over the universe they come.
They will dance; may you behold them.
A horse nation, they will dance,
May you behold them.

How Kwaku Ananse was Punished for his Bad Manners

Peggy Appiah

One year there had been no rain in the forest and everything was so dry that there was no food in Ananse's village. He and his family went hungry; they searched in vain for something to eat.

Now Ananse's son, Ntikuma, was growing up and was able to go and hunt for himself. One day, wandering far from the village, he came upon a big hole in the ground, and there, lying near it, were three large nuts. Now Ntikuma was very hungry and realising that three nuts would not feed a family he decided to eat them himself and then go on with his search for food.

He cracked the first one carefully on a stone but it shot out of the shell and bounced into the big hole. He tried the second one, being more careful, but somehow the nut eluded him and rolled down the hole. In despair he took the third nut and swore that if he did not eat it he would go down into the hole and look for the nuts. Sure enough when the shell split the nut shot up into the air, over Ntikuma's shoulder and into the hole. He stood up and made for the hole.

Now the hole was dark and deep, but Ntikuma did not lack courage and, making himself a rope of creepers, he climbed down into the hole. To his surprise it became lighter at the bottom, and he climbed off the rope into another land.

An old woman was sitting nearby, eating nuts by the door of her hut. He greeted her politely.

'Why have you come here?' she asked.

'I was looking for food, Grandmother,' he said. 'I found three nuts but they all rolled into this hole and I came down after them.'

The old woman stared at Ntikuma, saw he was telling the truth and spoke again. 'Go behind the house. There is a big farm there and there are plenty of yams. Go and collect some, but the ones which say "Take me" do not touch, only those which say "Do not take me". Bring me some of those and we will cook some – the others you shall take home.'

Ntikuma went into the farm and did exactly as he was told. He left the yams which asked to be taken strictly alone, and waited to find those which told him to leave them alone. At last he found these and collecting as many as he could carry he brought them back to the old lady. By now she had a fire ready and handing Ntikuma a knife she said: 'Peel off the outside carefully and put it in the pot. The inside throw away.' Ntikuma did as he was told and soon a wonderful smell came from the fire. When the meal was ready the old lady asked Ntikuma to sit down with her and gave him a bowl of food. It was delicious. Ntikuma ate quickly as he was hungry. Then he sat back to watch the old woman. He saw that she was eating through her nose. He was far too polite to remark on this and just sat and waited until she had finished. Then he said he must go home, and begged to take some yams to his mother. These the old lady willingly gave him, but first she told him to go into her room. There he would find two drums, one big and one small. He was to take the small one home with him. This he did, thanking the old woman warmly for her gifts. She told him that when he was hungry he had to only to say 'Cover' to the drum and food would come. So he went home to his family rejoicing.

Ntikuma told the whole story to his family after they had had the first good meal for days. His father, being jealous of his son's success, said he would go the next day and bring back something even better. He chided

his son for obeying so meekly the old woman who was obviously a witch and could have given him more.

Early the next day Ananse went off to try his hand. So good were Ntikuma's directions that he easily found the spot and saw three nuts lying by the hole. 'I will follow the nuts into the hole,' he said. He cracked them right near the edge but instead of rolling in they seemed determined to stay outside. In the end he had to push the last nut in. The rope Ntikuma had made was still there and he climbed down into the hole.

Sure enough there was the old woman eating nuts. Ananse looked at her and said, 'My, what an ugly old woman you are.' But the old lady took no notice of him and went on eating nuts. Then she asked him why he had come to see her. 'Why to get food of course,' said Ananse. 'If you can give my son much, why then you must be able to give me more.'

The old lady looked at him and smiled. 'If you are so sure, then go behind the house. There is a farm there and there are plenty of yams. Do not take the ones which say "Take me" but only those which say "Do not take me".'

Ananse replied, 'I am sure you are cheating me. I shall take which I please.' And he stumped off into the farm.

The first yam he saw was an enormous one. 'Take me, take me,' it cried. Ananse immediately went and cut it. But when he cut it open he found that it was full of hard nuts. Then he went further into the farm and finally found the yams which said 'Do not take me', and collected a pile and took them back to the cottage.

The old lady had a pot boiling on the fire. She said to Ananse, 'Peel the yams carefully and throw away the inside, boiling the outside.'

Ananse was angry. 'What do you take me for?' he said. 'One always cooks the inside of the yam.' And he put the inside of the yam in the pot and threw away the skin. He came back and looked in the pot and saw that it was full of stones. He had thrown the skins away, so he was forced to go to the farm and collect more yams, and to the stream and collect more water for the pot.

Then he did as the old woman said.

At last they sat down to their meal. Ananse stared at the old woman, seeing she was eating through her nose. 'What a filthy habit,' he said. 'Why do you eat through your nose?' Then he laughed and laughed at the old woman. But she kept silent. Soon he pushed back his stool and said that he must go home.

The old woman watched him collect his pile of yams and then said to him, 'Before you go, go into my room. You will find two drums, one big and one small. Take the small one home with you.'

Ananse went into the old lady's room and saw a very beautiful big drum and a small plain one. I am not going to take the small one, he thought. The big one will probably give me gold as well as food. So he lifted the big one on his shoulder and without giving another look at the old woman, climbed up the rope and went home.

It was with pride that Ananse put the big drum on the floor of his hut. He told the others to gather round and look at it. Then, fearing that they might take whatever treasure it produced, he asked them to go and fetch wood and water so that they could have a feast. Aso his wife and Ntikuma willingly went out to look for wood and water, wondering what wonders they would see on their return.

Kwaku Ananse sat down in front of the drum, admiring its carvings. He went to the door to make sure no one was about. Then he sat, and said in a loud voice, 'Cover.'

Alas and alack, Kwaku Ananse had taken the wrong drum. As soon as he had pronounced the magic word there was not a wonderful meal, there was not gold nor treasures, but Ananse himself saw with horror that his whole body was covered with sores and scabs. He was not fit to be seen. He cried out and ran from the house. The drum, having completed its task, disappeared. The family searched and searched for Ananse, but knowing his greed they took it for granted he had gone off to enjoy his treasure alone. It was not for many months that he returned home, bearing for always the scars of his many sores and remaining remarkably silent about his drum.

From *Tales of an Ashanti Father*

What the children said:

'He shouldn't have laughed at the old lady. It served him right that he ended up horrible to look at.'

'I liked it because he'd been bad and got punished.'

The Ski-Race

Alf Proysen

Mrs Pepperpot has done a lot of things in her life, and most of them I've told you about already. But now I must tell you how she went ski-racing one day last winter . . .

Mr Pepperpot had decided to go in for the annual local ski-race. He had been a pretty good skier when he was young, so he said to Mrs Pepperpot:

'I don't see why I shouldn't have a go this year; I feel more fit than I have for many years.'

'That's right, husband, you do that,' said Mrs Pepperpot, 'and if you win the cup you'll get your favourite ginger cake when you come home.'

So Mr Pepperpot put his name down, and when the day came he put on his white anorak and blue cap with a bobble on the top and strings under his chin. He slung his skis over his shoulders and said he would wax them when he got to the starting point.

'Righto! Best of luck!' said Mrs Pepperpot. She was already greasing the cake-tin and stoking the stove for her baking.

'Thanks, wife,' said Mr Pepperpot and went off. It was not before he had turned the corner by the main road that Mrs Pepperpot caught sight of his tin of wax which he had left on the sideboard.

'What a dunderhead that man is!' exclaimed Mrs Pepperpot. 'Now I shall have to go after him, I suppose; otherwise his precious skis are more likely to go backwards than forwards and there'll be no cup in this house today.'

So Mrs Pepperpot flung her shawl round her shoulders and trotted up the road as fast as she could with the tin of wax. When she got near the starting point there was a great crowd gathered. She dodged in and out to try and find her husband, but everyone seemed to be wearing white anoraks and blue caps. At last she saw a pair of sticks stuck in the snow with a blue cap hanging from the top. She could see the initials P.P. sewn in red thread inside.

That must be his cap, thought Mrs Pepperpot. Those are his initials, Peter Pepperpot. I sewed them on myself in red thread like that. I'll just drop the wax in the cap; then he'll find it when he comes to pick up his sticks.

As she bent forward to put the wax in the cap she accidentally knocked it off the stick and at that moment she shrank so quickly that it was she who fell into the cap, while the tin of wax rolled out into the snow!

No harm done, thought Mrs Pepperpot; when he comes along he'll see me in his cap. Then he can put me down somewhere out of the way of the race. And as soon as I grow large again I can go home.

But a moment later a big hand reached down, snatched up the cap and crammed it over a mop of thick hair. The strings were firmly tied and Mrs Pepperpot was trapped!

Oh well! she thought. I'd better not say anything before the race starts. For she knew Mr Pepperpot hated to think anybody might get to know about her shrinking.

'Number 46!' she heard the starter shout. 'On your mark, get set, go!' And Number 46, with Mrs Pepperpot in his cap, glided off to a smooth start.

Somebody must have lent him some wax, she thought; there's nothing wrong with his skis, anyway. Then from under the cap she shouted, 'Don't overdo it, now, or you'll have no breath left for the spurt at the end!'

She could feel the skier slow up a little. 'I suppose you know who's under your cap? she added. 'You had forgotten the wax, so I brought it along. Only I fell into your cap instead of the wax.'

Mrs Pepperpot now felt the skier's head turn round to see if anyone was talking to him from behind.

'It's me, you fool!' said Mrs Pepperpot. 'I've shrunk again. You'll have to put me off by the lane to our house – you pass right by, remember?'

But the skier had stopped completely now.

'Come on, man, get a move on!' shouted Mrs Pepperpot. 'They'll all be passing you!'

'Is it . . . is it true that you're the little old woman who shrinks to the size of a pepperpot?'

'Of course – you know that!' laughed Mrs Pepperpot.

'Am I married to *you*? Is it *my* wife who shrinks?'

'Yes, yes, but hurry now!'

'No,' said the skier, 'if that's how it is I'm not going on with the race at all.'

'Rubbish!' shouted Mrs Pepperpot. 'You *must* go on! I put a cake in the oven before I went out and if it's scorched it'll be all your fault!'

But the skier didn't budge.

'Maybe you'd like me to pop out of your cap and show myself to everybody? Any minute now I might go back to my full size and then the cap will burst and the whole crowd will see who is married to the shrinking woman. Come on, now! With any luck you may just do it, but there's no time to lose; HURRY!'

This worked; the skier shot off at full speed, helping himself to huge strides with his sticks. 'Fore!' he shouted as he sped past the other skiers. But when they came to the refreshment stall Mrs Pepperpot could smell the lovely hot soup, and she thought her husband deserved a break. 'We're well up now,' she called. 'You could take a rest.'

The skier slowed down to a stop and Mrs Pepperpot could hear there were many people standing round him. 'Well done!' they said. 'You're very well placed. But what are you looking so worried about? Surely you're not frightened of the last lap, are you?'

'No, no, nothing like that!' said the skier. 'It's this cap of mine – I'm dead scared of my cap!'

But the people patted him on the back and told him not to worry, he had a good chance of winning.

Under the cap Mrs Pepperpot was getting restless again. 'That's enough of that!' she called. 'We'll have to get on now!'

The people who stood nearest heard the voice and wondered who spoke. The woman who ladled out the soup said, 'Probably some loud-speaker.'

And Mrs Pepperpot couldn't help laughing. 'Nearer the truth than you think!' she thought. Then she called out again, 'Come on, husband, put that spurt on, and let's see if we can make it!'

And the skis shot away again, leaping many yards each time the sticks struck into the snow. Very soon Mrs Pepperpot could hear the sound of clapping and cheering.

'What do we do now?' whispered the skier in a miserable voice. 'Can you last another minute? Then I can throw the cap off under the fir trees just before we reach the finishing line.'

'Yes, that will be all right,' said Mrs Pepperpot. And, as the skis sped down the last slope, the strings were untied and the cap flew through the air, landing safely under the fir trees.

When Mrs Pepperpot had rolled over and over many times she found herself growing big once more. So she got up, shook the snow off her skirt and walked quietly home to her house. From the cheering in the distance she was sure her husband had won the cup.

The cake was only a little bit burnt on the top when she took it out of the oven, so she cut off the black part and gave it to the cat. Then she whipped some cream to put on top and made a steaming pot of coffee to have ready for her champion husband.

Sure enough, Mr Pepperpot soon came home – *without* the cup. 'I forgot to take the wax,' he said, 'so I didn't think it was worth going in for the race. But I watched it, and you should have seen Paul Petersen today; I've never seen him run like that in all my born days. All the same, he looked very queer, as if he'd seen a ghost or something. When it was over he kept talking about his wife and his cap, and he wasn't satisfied till he'd telephoned his house and made sure his wife had been there all the time, watching the race on television.'

Then Mrs Pepperpot began to laugh. And ever since, when she's feeling sad or things are not going just right, all she has to do is to remember the day she went ski-racing in the wrong cap, and then she laughs and laughs and laughs.

From *Mrs Pepperpot to the Rescue*

What the children said:

'I liked it when she changed back and found she had been in the wrong cap.'

'I liked it when Mr Pepperpot said he was just watching it.'

Two Giants

Edna O'Brien

Finn was the biggest and the bravest giant in all of Ireland. His deeds were known far and wide, lions lay down before him, his chariot flashed like a comet through the fields of battle, and with his 'Venomous' Sword he lay low a hundred men while with the other hand casting his sling at a troop of deer or a herd of wild boar. Along with that he had a thumb of knowledge and when he sucked this thumb he could tell what was happening anywhere in Ireland and he could foretell the future encounters. Now when Finn was no longer young, the rumour went about that there was a giant in Scotland who was Finn's equal and his name was McConigle. McConigle was not only fierce in battle, but when he walked up a hill the earth trembled under his feet, the trees wobbled, and the wild game fled to their lairs. By one blow of his fist he flattened a thunderbolt one day, turned it into the shape of a pancake and kept it in his pocket as a souvenir. He too had a way of prophesising by putting his middle finger into his mouth and sucking on it. Now the giants had never met but it was reported that McConigle intended to come over to Ireland, to fight Finn and to give him a pasting.

It so happened that one day Finn and his men were away from home and were busy making a bridge across the Giant's Causeway. In the distance they could see a messenger galloping towards them and Finn wondered if his wife Oonagh had taken sick or if there had been some breach in their fortifications at home. The messenger announced that Finn was to come home at once and then whispered something in Finn's ear that made him tremble with rage.

'So he's on my trail,' said Finn as he stood up and with that he pulled up a big fir tree, banged the clay off it and with his knife snedded it into a walking stick, so that it was both a walking stick and an umbrella. To see Finn walk was like seeing a mountain move and in no time he was across one county and heading towards home. He was going up a slope when in the mud he saw footmarks which were as big as his own. In fact they were the exact shape as his own and Finn thought, Lo, and had his first feeling of terror and doubt. Never before had he come across a giant the length and breadth of whose feet were as enormous as his own. He widened his chest and let out an almighty roar just to make his presence felt and it echoed all over the valley and was heard by his wife in her own home.

Finn's palace was on the top of a hill called Knockmany and it looked out on another mountain called Culamore and there was a deep gorge in between. Finn had settled there so that he could see his enemies a long way off and as well as that he could throw the bodies of his prey into the gorge for the crows to fatten themselves on.

'Oh my bilberry,' said Finn as he saw his wife Oonagh who had plaited her hair and put on a silk dress to please him. At once Finn asked if the reason she had sent for him was true.

'Tis true, Avick,' said Oonagh and went on to tell him how McConigle had pitched tent at the far side of the province and had his famous thunderbolt in the shape of a pancake in his pocket, and called himself The Invincible. Finn put his thumb into his mouth to verify all these things and found that they were true. He could only use his gift of prophecy on very trying and solemn occasions such as this was.

'Finn darling, don't bite your thumb,' said Oonagh

very sweetly as she led him into the house where there was a dinner prepared. Finn squatted at one end of the low table, Oonagh at the other, and along with maidens to wait on them there were harpists playing in order to soothe Finn. He started by having sixteen duck eggs, eight pig's crubeens and three raw onions for his digestion. The main course was a haunch of roast venison and it was so long that it stretched between them down the length of the table, a sizzling roast dotted with berries and all sorts of herbs. But no matter how much he ate or drank there was a frown on Finn's forehead and a big brown ridge like a furrow on the bridge of his nose because of his thinking.

'Dearest,' said Oonagh as she bobbed along and began to stroke his great naked back. Finn always removed his cloak before he sat down to eat.

'You'll best him, you always do,' said Oonagh, but Finn shook his head and said it was perilous because according to his thumb he and McConigle had equal amounts of strength, ate the same amount of food, weighed the same, and were equally matched in daring, wisdom and cunning.

'What else does it say?' Oonagh asked and Finn put his thumb right inside his mouth and shut his eyes in order to concentrate.

· 'Take care you don't draw blood,' said Oonagh.

'He's coming,' said Finn, 'he's below in Dungannon,' and at that he jumped up.

'When will he be here?' said Oonagh.

'He'll be here before long,' said Finn and he began to put his vest and his jacket on. He looked at his wife and for the first time she saw fear and apprehension in his eyes. She decided that she would have to help him and

make use of her own enchantments. Oonagh was in
with the fairies too and with her wand had once turned
a hussy into a hound. She told Finn that she would help
him to succeed.

'How, how,' said Finn, hitting the table and sending
delph in all directions.

Oonagh hurried out of the doorway in order to give a
message to her sister who lived on the opposite

mountain at Culamore.

'Grania,' said Oonagh, 'are you at home?'

'I'm in the kitchen garden,' said Grania, 'I'm picking berries for a tart.'

'Run up to the top of the hill and look about you and tell us if you see anything untoward,' said Oonagh. They waited for a few minutes with Finn pacing up and down and servants fanning him with great leaves.

'I am there now,' said Grania.

'What do you see?' said Oonagh.

'Oh lawsie me,' exclaimed Grania, 'I see the biggest giant I've ever seen coming out of the town of Dungannon.'

'What is he like?' said Oonagh.

'He's something terrible to behold,' said Grania and went on to describe a giant of about twelve feet in height, his hair all the way down to his waist, his face ruddy like any giant's except that he had daubed blood over it and, most unnerving of all, his three eyes. He had an eye in the middle of his head that was rolling round like the hands of a clock. Not only was the ground shaking beneath him but the birds in the trees were dying of fright. Along with that he was laughing out loud as if he had just heard the most hilarious joke.

'He's coming up to leather Finn,' said Oonagh to her sister.

'Finn has my sympathy,' said Grania and then she just announced that the giant had picked up a white goat and was wringing its neck and was obviously going to eat it raw.

'I'll tell you what,' said Oonagh, 'call down to him and invite him up to your place for a bite to eat.'

'Why so?' said Finn, unable to follow his wife's drift

74

of thought.

'Strategy,' said Oonagh, 'strategy.'

Grania called across to say she'd be glad to oblige and she'd entertain the monster but she was a bit short of bacon and of butter.

'I'll fling you some across,' said Oonagh and she snapped her fingers for a servant to bring a flitch of bacon and a firkin of butter. However, before throwing them she forgot to say her charms and didn't the butter and the bacon fall into a stream and get carried away.

'Never mind,' said Grania, 'I'll give him heather soup and I'll put shredded bark in it to give him indigestion.'

'Good on you,' said Oonagh and she winked at Finn.

'He'll skewer me,' said Finn.

'Don't be ridiculous,' said Oonagh although to tell you the truth she could see a situation where she herself might be a dainty morsel, a little fritter for the giant's supper.

'My courage is leaving me, I'll be disgraced,' said Finn.

'Two heads are better than one,' said Oonagh as she went towards the place where she kept her magic threads. She drew nine woollen threads of different colours, she plaited them into three plaits, with three colours in each one; she put a plait on her right arm, another round her right ankle, a third round her heart, and in that way Oonagh was protected. Then she got going. She asked the servants to go up in the loft and bring down iron griddles and a child's cradle. She got them to make cakes but she hid the griddles inside the cakes and then baked them in the fire in the usual way. When they were done she dusted them over with flour so as to hide any protuberances and she put them in the window to cool. Then she put down a large pot of milk which she later made into curds and whey and showed Finn how to pick up a curd in his hand and make it smooth as a stone. Then she got a nightgown and a shawl and dressed Finn in it and put a nightcap on his head. She told him that he would have to get into the cradle and completely cover himself with clothes, with only his two eyes peering out.

'I can't fit in a cradle,' said Finn.

'You'll have to double up,' said Oonagh.

'I'll have to triple up,' said Finn as she pushed him towards it.

'You must pass for your own child,' said Oonagh.

'But I'm not a child,' said Finn and he was afraid that he had taken the cowardice too far. Oonagh ignored his mutterings and just put him into the cradle and covered him up with great wool blankets and red deerskins.

'What do I do?' said Finn.

'Whist,' said Oonagh because they could hear the bruiser coming up the hill and giving a skelp of his axe to the dogs to shut them up. He strutted across the courtyard and when he arrived at their door he put a hand around either oak pillar and bellowed:

'Anyone home?'

Oonagh came forward all shy and mincing and gave a little gasp to signify to him how formidable he was. He had rat skins and coon skins dangling from his ears and his third eye was rolling about like a spinning top.

'Mr McConigle,' said Oonagh.

'The great McConigle,' said the giant and then asked if he was in the house of Finn.

'Indeed you are,' said Oonagh and gestured towards a chair to make him welcome.

'You're Mrs Finn I suppose,' said the giant.

'I am,' said she, 'and a proud wife at that.'

'Thinks he's the toughest giant in Ireland,' said McConigle.

'It's a proven fact,' said his wife proudly.

'There's a man within three feet of you that's very desirous of having a tussle with him,' said McConigle and he looked around in order to sniff out his rival.

'Is he hiding from me?' he asked.

'Hiding?' said Oonagh. 'He left here frothing, he's gone out to find you and it's lucky for you didn't meet him, or you'd be a dead man now, your head on his pike as an ornament.'

'You vixen,' said McConigle and he roared with rage but Oonagh was in no way dismayed.

'He's twice your height and much better built,' said she.

'You don't know my strength,' said McConigle.

'In that case would you turn the house,' said Oonagh.

The giant stood up, put his middle finger in his mouth, thought for an instant, then went out, put his arms around the house, picked it up and put it facing a different way. Finn in his cradle was now facing in a different direction and there was sweat pouring out of him with heat and nerves.

'You're a handy giant,' said Oonagh and then told him that she was short of water, but that there was a fine spring under some rocks and that if he could split the rocks she'd be most obliged. He took his axe out from under his leather apron, struck at the rocks and tore a cleft that was hundreds of feet deep. Oonagh began to have doubts.

'Come in and eat,' said she and added that although her husband would make mince of him, the laws of hospitality must be observed.

She placed before him six cakes of the bread and a mound of newly churned butter and she sat down pretending to be polite. He put one of the cakes in his mouth, took a bite and let out the most terrible growl.

'What kind of bread is this,' he said fiercely.

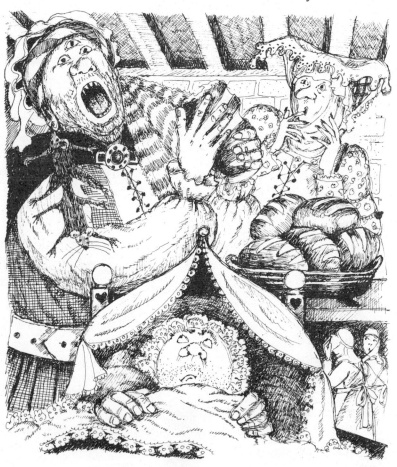

'Fresh bread,' said Oonagh, cool as a breeze.

'And here are two teeth of mine gone,' said he as he hauled out two big molars that were grey in colour and shaped like drinking horns.

'Why,' said Oonagh, 'that's Finn's bread, the only bread that he eats, him and the child there.' At that she offered another cake. As soon as he put it in his mouth another great crack was heard and he let out a yell far fiercer than the first, so that the baby mewled. 'Thunder and giblets,' said he as he pulled out two more teeth with bits of gum on them.

'Well, Mr McConigle,' said Oonagh, 'if you can't manage the bread, don't bother with it but don't be disturbing my child.'

'Mammy, mammy, can I have some bread,' said the baby from the cradle and its voice gave McConigle a start. Oonagh very cleverly handed a cake that had no griddle in and McConigle was flabbergasted as he watched the child gobble it up.

'I'd like to take a glimpse at that lad in the cradle,' said he.

'Certainly,' said Oonagh and she told the little baby to get up and prove himself the worthy child of his father. Now the baby stood up, looked at McConigle and said, 'Are you as strong as me?'

'Thundering giblets,' said McConigle, 'how dare you insult me.'

'Can you squeeze water out of a stone?' said the child, and he put a stone into McConigle's hand. McConigle squeezed and squeezed but not a drop of liquid came out.

'Watch me,' said the child and he put his hands under the covers, took out one of the white curds that looked exactly like a stone and squeezed until the liquid came out in a little shower from his hands.

'My daddy is training me,' said he, 'but I have a lot to learn yet.'

McConigle was speechless.

'I'll go back to sleep now,' said the child, 'but I'd hate to waste my time on anyone that hasn't my daddy's strength, that can't eat daddy's bread or squeeze water out of a stone.' Then he slipped down and as Oonagh was pulling the covers up over him he raised his index finger and gave a word of warning to McConigle. 'I'd be off out of here if I were you as it's in flummery my father will have you.'

'What he says is a fact,' said Oonagh as she tucked Finn into the cradle and patted him to let him know how proud she was.

'I'm thinking it is,' said McConigle.

'You're not in his league at all,' said Oonagh and went on to remind McConigle that if the child was that strong he could only guess at the immensity of the father.

'Will you let me feel the teeth of that infant?' said he still in a quandry.

'By all means,' said Oonagh and she took his hand and she stuck it straight into Finn's mouth explaining that the child's best teeth were in the back of his head. McConigle was amazed to find a baby with a full set of grinders and more amazed when he felt something snap and then felt his finger detach itself and when he pulled out his hand there was a big wound where his finger of knowledge had been. Finn had eaten it. So shocked was he and so horror-stricken that he fell down. Finn rose from the cradle and laid roundly on the monster with his bare hands. He could easily have killed him with his sword but that McConigle begged for his life and Finn being a chivalrous hero gave it to him. After that McConigle made his peace, picked up his teeth and his accroutrements and promised to go home to Scotland and never set foot in Ireland again.

From *Tales for the Telling: Irish Folk and Fairy Stories*

What the children said:

'It was bloodthirsty, it was very good.'

'Good, funny, mega-brilliant.'

Quaka Raja

Grace Hallworth

There was once a poor widow who lived in a hut at the edge of the forest with her four children.

She favoured her three daughters – Minnie Minnie, Minnie Bitana, and Philambo – but she did not care a wit for her son, Quaka Raja. Yet Quaka Raja was obedient and worked hard in the vegetable garden in front of the hut while his three sisters quarrelled and fought among themselves all day. They made fun of Quaka because he was kind to the birds and animals of the forest, and always saved some of his food for them.

Every Friday the widow set out for the village market where she sold the vegetables and fruit from her garden. Everyone flocked to buy her dasheen, yams, sweet potatoes, mangoes, sapodillas, peas and beans, and soon her basket was empty. With the money she received she bought food to take home and filled her basket with all manner of goodies. There was arape, a cornmeal pancake with spicy meat filling, molasses balls, sugar cakes, black pudding, and many other things besides.

When she returned to the little hut she stood outside and sang:

'Minnie Minnie, come here,
Minnie Bitana, come here,
Philambo, come here,
Leave Quaka Raja one dey.'

As soon as the three daughters heard the song they ran to unlock the door, pushing Quaka Raja aside as the mother did not want him. Then the food was shared. but Quaka Raja's portion was always the least of all.

Now in the forest lived a man called Zobolak who

was feared by all the villagers. He was a hideous-looking creature, with a deeply scarred face, fiery red eyes, and arms and legs that were huge and round, with clawlike hands and feet. Mothers warned their children to keep away from the forest, for whenever a child disappeared it was whispered that Zobolak had stolen it, though no one could prove this was true.

One Friday, when the widow returned from market, Zobolak, who had been hunting agouti, happened to be nearby. Peeping through the bushes he heard the widow's song and saw the three daughters run out to greet their mother. Zobolak could hardly restrain himself from rushing forward and seizing the three girls then and there, but he was as cunning as the wild animals which he hunted in the forest. He settled down to wait.

The next Friday the widow again set out for market. After some time had passed, Zobolak crept up to the hut and sang in a high voice:

> *'Minnie Minnie, come here,*
> *Minnie Minnie, come here,*
> *Minnie Minnie, come here,*
> *Leave Quaka Raja one dey.'*

The three daughters ran to open the door, but Quaka Raja said, 'Sisters, sisters, do not go out. That is not Mamma's song.' And he stood in front of the door and would not let them out even though they tugged and pulled until they were exhausted.

When the children did not open the door, Zobolak hid in the forest until the mother returned. But he stayed close by to listen carefully to the song.

84

The following Friday the mother set off once more for the village, and after a little while Zobolak crept up to the hut and sang in a high voice:

> 'Minnie Minnie, come here,
> Minnie Minnie, come here,
> Philambo, come here,
> Leave Quaka Raja one dey.'

The three daughters ran to unlock the door, but Quaka Raja said, 'Sisters, sisters, do not go out. That is not Mamma's song.'

They tugged and pulled and scratched him but he stood fast in front of the door, and at last they fell down exhausted.

Once more Zobolak crept away into the forest when they did not open the door, but he waited close by until the mother returned.

At last Friday came. Zobolak's eyes gleamed with excitement as he waited. No sooner had the widow left than he crept up to the hut and sang in a high voice:

> 'Minnie Minnie, come here,
> Minnie Bitana, come here,
> Philambo, come here,
> Leave Quaka Raja one dey.'

Quaka Raja stood in front of the door and begged his sisters not to go out. The mother had just left. How could she be back so soon? But they tugged and pulled and scratched and kicked him so hard that he fell to the ground, senseless.

They ran out to greet their mother, but –

'Ayayayayay!' – there was Zobolak waiting for them. He threw them into his sack, slung it over his shoulder and off he went into the forest where he lived.

By the time Quaka Raja came to his senses Zobolak was far, far away. Quaka Raja ran hither and yon calling his sisters, but only the birds cheeped back at him. When his mother returned from the village and he told her what had happened, she was wild with grief. But Quaka Raja said, 'Do not cry, Mamma, I will go and look for my sisters and bring them back to you.'

At first his mother begged him not to go. 'Son, you are all that I have now,' she said; 'I cannot lose you too.'

But Quaka Raja pleaded with her until she agreed. So she packed him some of the food she had brought back and sent him off with tears in her eyes.

Quaka walked long and he walked far. He walked all day, and as night fell he saw a light in the distance. As he approached it he came to a hut half hidden by trees and creepers. Inside he could hear his sisters crying.

What to do? He could not rescue them without help. As he stood under a tree thinking, an owl overhead hooted and nearly frightened him out of his wits. At that moment he thought of a plan. He could ask his friends, the birds and animals of the forest, to help him.

Much later that night, as the moon climbed down behind the mountain, the stillness of the forest was shattered by a horrible noise. Zobolak was startled out of his sleep as the sound grew louder and louder and came nearer and nearer, like the shrieks of a hundred demons coming after him. He rushed out of his hut like a hunted animal and ran deep into the forest, over the mountains, anywhere away from that terrible noise.

What was that noise? It was the sound of owls

hooting, frogs croaking, wild cats yowling, wild pigs snoring and grunting, parrots screaming and birds chirping and whistling. They had all come to help Quaka Raja.

So Quaka Raja returned home with his sisters and his mother was so proud of him that if he weren't such a sensible child he would have been thoroughly spoiled.

And for all we know Zobolak is still running!

From *Listen to this Story*

What the children said:

'The goodies won in the end. I like those sort of stories.'

'I'm glad Quaka Raja's mother loved him in the end.'

Wambu the Duck

Rene Beckley

In the Dreamtime the great god Baiame made everything, and he liked what he made for he saw it was good. He made the mountains and the plains, the sea and the sky. After he had finished marking in the river-beds with his huge spear, he caused his magic rain to fall gently, so as not to frighten the people. The great rain soon filled the rivers.

He showed the tribespeople how to hunt with spears just like his own. He gave them fire to cook their food and to warm them when the cold winds blew, or when chilly night air made them shiver.

Then with the lovely world complete Baiame went up to rest in Bullima the Sky-Camp to watch his people and animals live out their lives in the good land he had made.

He sat gazing joyfully over the whole earth, pleased that at last he could rest from his labours. All at once his gaze rested on the lower hills in a certain part of the land, where there was a sparkling billabong, colourful with scarlet water-lilies and fringed with sweet crisp grass.

'Ah, there is Wumbulgal,' he said to himself, for the great god Baiame knew even the smallest duck in the land. 'Now let us see what Wumbulgal will make of her life.' He sat gazing at the little duck.

Wumbulgal was a young duck who lived on one of Baiame's lovely billabongs. She was a very pretty little duck with a pretty name. Her friends all loved her because she was so happy and gay, and she swam and dived and flew so well. Because she was so friendly and jolly she was soon called Wambu for short – it was easier than her own long name.

As she was such a good swimmer she often paddled

90

off on her own to explore the billabong. She loved to be by herself, but often she found herself in trouble with the older ducks of her tribe for swimming so far alone.

The other ducks were too frightened to swim as far as Wambu, for they were all afraid of dreadful Muloca the Water Devil, who lurked in the green depths down the river.

Not only did Muloca live in those deep unknown waters, but also the very water itself was dangerous, for it was muddy and thick with weeds, and the current was strong enough to drown little ducks like Wambu. There, too, in that horrid part of the river, so much feared by the duck tribe, lived many fierce water rats.

But Wambu was not afraid of Water Devils or Rats, she was far too busy enjoying herself, and even Baiame away in the great distance saw her delight.

It was a very hot day, so Wambu paddled lazily through the cool shining waters hardly moving her webbed feet, cooling herself idly, and not going anywhere in particular. All at once she saw some lovely young green shoots of tender grass in the distance. She swam off to gather them, going further down the dark waters than even she intended.

She was tired after the long swim in the heat of the day, so she waddled up on to the bank to eat the grass. She had just filled her beak with the green shoots when two rough arms grabbed her. She struggled and kicked her webbed feet, she struggled and pushed with her wings, but Water Rat (for it was he who had caught her, not Muloca) was strong and fierce. He held her firmly in his big arms and soon pulled her into his burrow at the creek's edge.

She quacked and cried in distress, 'Let me go, let me

go, kind Rat!' but he would not release her. 'Please, please, Rat, let me go home to my family.'

'No, no, little Wambu. I have watched you many times swimming near my home. You are a very beautiful little duck, and I am very lonely. I must have a wife. You shall stay with me, always,' he said.

'No, no! Good, kind Water Rat. Let me go. I don't want to be your wife,' she replied.

'My name is Goomai. I am King of the Water Rats. It is fitting that I should have a wife different from the other rat wives. You shall stay. I very much desire a wife, but if you try to escape I will kill you with my spear.'

So poor Wambu argued no more. She was indeed very frightened of Goomai and he kept a strict guard on her with the spears he carried on his big hind legs.

Now Wambu had been very silly to swim so far and be caught by Goomai, but now when she was in real trouble for the first time, she soon became sensible. 'I must escape,' she said to herself. 'Oh, I am very, very frightened of the horrid rat, but I'm not too frightened to plan an escape. I must escape. I will escape!'

So Wambu watched and waited her chance to leave the burrow, always pretending she enjoyed being Goomai's wife. Many, many times during the days that followed, did she hear the calls of her tribespeople as they searched for her, but always Goomai guarded her. 'You shall not leave me, Wambu,' he would growl.

'No, kind Goomai,' she would quack her soft reply.

Only at night would he let her out of his creekside burrow, when he was sure there was no one near, and she would be afraid to swim away in the dark.

Wambu was such a clever little duck that she soon

convinced her husband she was really happy with him, so eventually he returned to his old habit of sleeping in the daytime.

He slept thus for several weeks and each time he awoke, there was the little duck, soft, fluffy and warm, still faithfully by his side.

At last Wumbulgal plucked up courage one afternoon while Goomai slept. Quickly she swam away to the mouth of the burrow and out into the billabong until at last she was able to paddle off downstream. Terrified Goomai would follow her, she swam and dived frantically until she reached her old home.

Her tribe gabbled and quacked excitedly. 'Here is Wambu! Look, see, here is Wambu!' they cried.

Wambu told her story to the accompaniment of quacks from her friends. 'So you see, all you ducks, the foolishness of swimming too far from home. Let this be a lesson to you. Do not stray from your own homes.' For Wambu had learnt by her folly that what the older ducks had told her was true.

She was so happy, she wiggled her tail and splashed her wings and dived and kicked and swam. Every day she swam in the billabong, and by night she flew in the light of Baalu, but always close to her home.

Soon came the time for the ducks to nest and lay their eggs. A busy time it was of waddling feet and jostling feathers; of busy beaks pushing reeds into place in the nests, in bushes and reeds and in hollow trees. How peaceful then it became on the billabong with each duck sitting patiently on her eggs, waiting for the ducklings to push their way through the brittle shells. Wambu too, laid her eggs in a clump of reeds she had lined most carefully with soft feathers and grasses.

At last the day arrived when the little ducklings broke through their shells, and the parent ducks were able to take the little ducklings in to the creek for the first time. Big ducks with fluffy ducklings behind bobbed on the waters.

Wumbulgal too, sat on her nest until her eggs burst to disclose the ducklings, then she swam happily into the middle of the waters with her two young things paddling behind.

Immediately the other ducks quacked loudly with amusement, for they were very queer ducklings indeed these little ones of Wambu's. 'Just look at Wambu's babies! What peculiar children she has!' they cried unkindly.

She was more than a little annoyed by the unkind laughter. Admittedly her children were different, but they were still very lovely babies, with their soft brown fur. 'They are not like the other ducklings, but they are nice. Why do my people laugh?' Wambu could not understand.

There her ducklings were, floating on the waters: with soft brown fur instead of feathers; four webbed feet instead of two; with a sharp little point on each back leg just like the spears Goomai always carried. 'Oh dear!' sighed Wambu. Only their bills and feet were like a duck's, but the rest of the little creatures' bodies was very strange indeed.

Then suddenly the whole tribe of ducks took fright. they screamed and quacked at Wumbulgal. 'Take your babies away! Take them away, they are like that horrid Water Rat, Goomai. Look, they have his fur and they carry his spear on their hind legs. Take them away!'

'They will grow big like Goomai and kill our young,' shrilled another duck, hiding her babies under her wings.

'They may even grow big enough to kill us!' flapped another frightened mother.

'Take them away, take them away,' was the cry, 'or we will kill them.'

Poor Wambu! She was so proud of her little family, even if they were a little odd. But she was afraid that the ducks would carry out their threat to kill her young. Shall I go back to Goomai? she wondered. But no, he would only say the babies were not like him and he might want to kill them too. Besides, she disliked him so much – anything was better than living in his muddy burrow again.

She called her children. 'Come children, we will go away together.' So they paddled swiftly upstream towards the mountains, where no one knew them, to make a new home.

But always Wambu remained sad, for as the little ones grew up, they saw they were different, and kept to themselves, until poor Wambu became so lonely and unhappy she died.

So it was that the Gayadaree – for they were the first Platypus – lived on in the mountain creeks. They laid eggs and hatched out children two at a time, just like themselves, until a whole new tribe of animals emerged in the land Baiame had made.

And there in the mountain billabongs they remain – the Platypus, a tribe apart – for no duck had four legs, and no water rat ever laid eggs.

Baiame saw that it was good and he was pleased. Although Wumbulgal the duck died of grief, she had made a whole new tribe, and Baiame knew she would always be remembered with love by all who saw the Platypus.

From *Folk Tales of the World*

What the children said:

'A sad end for the brave duck.'

'I'd like to see a platypus.'

96

The People Could Fly

Virginia Hamilton

They say the people could fly. Say that long ago in Africa, some of the people knew magic. And they would walk up on the air like climbin up on a gate. And they flew like blackbirds over the fields. Black, shiny wings flappin against the blue up there.

Then, many of the people were captured for Slavery. The ones that could fly shed their wings. They couldn't take their wings across the water on the slave ships. Too crowded, don't you know.

The folks were full of misery, then. Got sick with the up and down of the sea. So they forgot about flyin when they could no longer breathe the sweet scent of Africa.

Say the people who could fly kept their power, although they shed their wings. They kept their secret magic in the land of slavery. They looked the same as the other people from Africa who had been coming over, who had dark skin. Say you couldn't tell anymore one who could fly from one who couldn't.

One such who could was an old man, call him Toby. And standin tall, yet afraid, was a young woman who once had wings. Call her Sarah. Now Sarah carried a babe tied to her back. She trembled to be so hard worked and scorned.

The slaves labored in the fields from sunup to sundown. The owner of the slaves callin himself their Master. Say he was a hard lump of clay. A hard, glinty coal. A hard rock pile, wouldn't be moved. His Overseer on horseback pointed out the slaves who were slowin down. So the one called Driver cracked his whip over the slow ones to make them move faster. That whip was a slice-open cut of pain. So they did move faster. Had to.

Sarah hoed and chopped the row as the babe on her back slept.

Say the child grew hungry. That babe started up bawling too loud. Sarah couldn't stop to feed it. Couldn't stop to soothe and quiet it down. She let it cry. She didn't want to. She had no heart to croon to it.

'Keep that thing quiet,' called the Overseer. He pointed his finger at the babe. The woman scrunched low. The Driver cracked his whip across the babe anyhow. The babe hollered like any hurt child, and the woman fell to the earth.

The old man that was there, Toby, came and helped her to her feet.

'I must go soon,' she told him.

'Soon,' he said.

Sarah couldn't stand up straight any longer. She was too weak. The sun burned her face. The babe cried and cried, 'Pity me, oh, pity me,' say it sounded like. Sarah was so sad and starvin, she sat down in the row.

'Get up, you black cow,' called the Overseer. He pointed his hand, and the Driver's whip snarled around Sarah's legs. Her sack dress tore into rags. Her legs bled onto the earth. She couldn't get up.

Toby was there where there was no one to help her and the babe.

'Now, before it's too late,' panted Sarah. 'Now, Father!'

'Yes, Daughter, the time is come,' Toby answered. 'Go, as you know how to go!'

He raised his arms, holding them out to her. '*Kum . . . yali, kum buba tambe,*' and more magic words, said so quickly, they sounded like whispers and sighs.

The young woman lifted one foot on the air. Then the

other. She flew clumsily at first, with the child now held tightly in her arms. Then she felt the magic, the African mystery. Say she rose just as free as a bird. As light as a feather.

The Overseer rode after her, hollerin. Sarah flew over the fences. She flew over the woods. Tall trees could not snag her. Nor could the Overseer. She flew like an eagle now, until she was gone from sight. No one dared speak about it. Couldn't believe it. But it was, because they that was there saw that it was.

Say the next day was dead hot in the fields. A young man slave fell from the heat. The Driver come and whipped him. Toby come over and spoke words to the fallen one. The words of ancient Africa once heard are never remembered completely. The young man forgot them as soon as he heard them. They went way inside him. He got up and rolled over on the air. He rode it awhile. And he flew away.

Another and another fell from the heat. Toby was there. He cried out to the fallen and reached his arms out to them. *'Kum kunka yali, kum . . . tambe!'* Whispers and sighs. And they too rose on the air. They rode the hot breezes. The ones flyin were black and shinin sticks, wheelin above the head of the Overseer. They crossed the rows, the fields, the fences, the streams, and were away.

'Seize the old man!' cried the Overseer. 'I heard him say the magic *words*. Seize him!'

The one callin himself Master come runnin. The Driver got his whip ready to curl around old Toby and tie him up. The slaveowner took his hip gun from its place. He meant to kill old, black Toby.

But Toby just laughed. Say he threw back his head

and said, 'Hee, hee! Don't you know who I am? Don't you know some of us in this field?' He said it to their faces. 'We are ones who fly!'

And he sighed the ancient words that were a dark promise. He said them all around to the others in the field under the whip. '. . . *buba yali* . . . *buba tambe* . . .'

There was a great outcryin. The bent backs straighted up. Old and young who were called slaves and could fly joined hands. Say like they would ring-sing. But they didn't shuffle in a circle. They didn't sing. They rose on the air. They flew in a flock that was black against the heavenly blue. Black crows or black shadows. It didn't matter, they went so high. Way above the plantation, way over the slavery land. Say they flew away to *Free-dom*.

And the old man, old Toby, flew behind them, takin care of them. He wasn't cryin. He wasn't laughin. He was the seer. His gaze fell on the plantation where the slaves who could not fly waited.

'*Take us with you!*' Their looks spoke it but they were afraid to shout it. Toby couldn't take them with him. Hadn't the time to teach them to fly. They must wait for a chance to run.

'Goodie-bye!' The old man called Toby spoke to them, pour souls! And he was flyin gone.

So they say. The Overseer told it. The one called Master said it was a lie, a trick of the light. The Driver kept his mouth shut.

The slaves who could not fly told about the people who could fly to their children. When they were free. When they sat close before the fire in the free land, they told it. They did so love firelight and *Free-dom* and tellin.

They say that the children of the ones who could not

fly told their children. And now, me, I have told it to you.

From *The People Could Fly: American Black Folktales*

What the children said:

'Very sad, I wanted to believe it.'

'It was great that the slaves could fly away from the cruel overseer.'

'The People Could Fly' is one of the most extraordinary, moving tales in black folklore. It almost makes us believe that the people *could* fly. There are numerous separate accounts of flying Africans and slaves in the black folktale literature. Such accounts are often combined with tales of slaves disappearing. A plausible explanation might be the slaves runing away from slavery, slipping away while in the fields or under cover of darkness. In code language murmured from one slave to another, 'Come fly away!' might have been the words used. Another explanation is the wish-fulfillment motif.

The magic hoe variant is often combined with the flying-African tale. A magic hoe is left still hoeing in an empty field after all the slaves have flown away. Magic with the hoe and other farm tools, and the power of disappearing, are often attributed to Gullah (Angolan) African slaves. Angolan slaves were thought by other slaves to have exceptional powers.

'The People Could Fly' is a detailed fantasy tale of suffering, of magic power exerted against the so-called Master and his underlings. Finally, it is a powerful testament to the millions of slaves who never had the opportunity to 'fly' away. They remained slaves, as did their children. 'The People Could Fly' was first told and retold by those who had only their imaginations to set them free.

Secrets

Anita Desai

One morning, at school, Rohan got every single sum wrong. Then he dropped a bottle of ink on the floor and it splashed on to his teacher's white canvas shoes. When he made a face behind his teacher's back, he was seen. So he had to be punished.

'Here, take this letter to your father and go home,' his teacher said, after writing a long and angry letter. 'Let him punish you as well.'

Rohan tried to look too proud to care, and picked up his books and walked out of the school yard and up the narrow city lane. But once he reached the big grey banyan tree that was the only tree in the lane, and found that the cobbler who usually sat under it, mending broken old shoes, was not there, he sat down in its shade, hiding himself in the folds of the great trunk, and sobbed a little with anger. He had not been able to get his sums right although he had tried. He had dropped the ink bottle by accident and not to spoil the teacher's white shoes. Perhaps it was bad of him to pull a face but how could he help it when things were going so badly? Now he was afraid to go home and hand the letter to his father, who would be very angry and beat him. He sometimes did, and often scolded him.

So Rohan hid there in the folds of the grey tree-trunk, and poked with a stick at the seeds dropped on the ground by the parrots that ate the red berries of the tree. He was so angry and afraid that he poked and poked with the stick till he had dug quite a deep hole in the dust. In that hole he found a little grey lump of rubber – a plain piece of rubber that some other schoolboy might have dropped there long ago. He picked it up and rolled it about between his fingers.

'I wish it were a magic rubber,' he said, sobbing a

little. 'I would rub out the whole school, like this – like this –' and he stepped out to look down the lane at the boys' school that stood at the end of it, and angrily rubbed at the air with the grey lump of rubber.

Then he stopped, his hand still in mid-air, his mouth still open, and his hair began to stand up on his head as it did on his neighbour's cat's back when she saw his dog.

Something very, very strange had happened. The school had vanished. He had really rubbed it out! The tall, three-storeyed house on its left, with its latticed balconies and green roof, was still there, and on the other side the tin-roofed warehouse where timber was stacked stood there too, but in between them, where the school had been, there was now a patch of earth. There was no white school building, no deep verandas, no dusty playground, no high grey wall and not a single schoolboy. There was just a square of bare brown earth between the other buildings, all quiet and still now in the heat of the afternoon.

Rohan's knees were shaking. He ran a little way down the road to see better but still could find nothing but a blank where the school had once been. Then he felt so afraid of the vanished school that he ran back up the lane as fast as he could, snatched up his books and the terrible rubber from among the roots of the banyan, and ran into the road where he lived. He hurried up the stairs at the side of the little yellow house to their room on the roof where his mother hung the clothes to dry and his father stacked old boxes and bicycle tyres.

His mother was alone at home. She was kneading dough in a big brass pan. The fire was not yet lit. 'You're early,' she said, in surprise. 'I haven't any food ready for you yet. But you can go and break up an old box and get me some wood to light the fire. I'll warm some milk for you. Hurry up, don't look so sulky,' she said, and began to roll and thump the dough in the pan, roll and thump, roll and thump, so she did not see the face Rohan made as he went out to pull an old crate to pieces and bring in an armload of packing-case wood.

He came in and threw it all into the grate with such force that the ashes and grit flew up and settled on all the pots and pans, and the dough and the neat floor as well.

His mother was so angry, she shouted, 'What's the matter with you, you rascal? Look what you've done! What a mess you've made! Now go and fetch the broom and sweep it up at once.'

'I won't sweep,' he shouted back, as loudly as though there were a devil in him, shouting for him.

She was still more angry. 'I won't sweep it up either. Let it lie there and then your father will see it when he comes home,' she said.

Then Rohan felt so afraid that he held up the magic rubber and cried, 'I won't let you do that. I won't let him see it. I'll – I'll rub you all out,' and he swept through the air with that little grey lump of rubber, as hard as he could. He shut his eyes tight because his face was all screwed up with anger, and when he opened them the whole house with the unlit fire, the brass pan, the glass of milk and even his mother had vanished. There was only the roof-top, blazing in the afternoon sun, littered with empty tins and old tyres at the edges but quite, quite bare in the middle.

Now Rohan did not have a home or a mother or even a glass of milk. His mouth hung open, he was so frightened by what he had done. Then he turned and ran down the stairs as fast as he could, so that his father would not come and find him standing alone on the empty roof-top.

He heard an excited bark and saw it was his dog Kalo, who had been sleeping in the shade of an overturned basket in a corner of the roof-top, but had heard him run down the stairs and followed him. Kalo was frightened, too, at the way their room had disappeared and the roof-top left standing empty, so he was running along behind Rohan, barking with fright.

Rohan felt afraid that the people who lived in the yellow house would come out and see what had happened, so he shouted, 'Go back Kalo! Go back!' But Kalo ran towards him, his long black ears flapping as he ran. So Rohan rubbed the air with his rubber again and screamed, 'I don't want you! Go away!' and Kalo vanished. His round paw marks were still to be seen in the dust of the road. A little trail of dust was still hanging in the hot, still air of that dreadful afternoon, but Kalo the dog had vanished.

And someone had seen. An old man who traded in empty tins and bottles had just started his evening round and, while shouting 'Tin and bo – ' stopped short and stared till Rohan, rubbing in the air with his rubber again, shouted, 'You can't see! You mustn't see!' and rubbed him out. That old man with his grey beard and big sack of clanking tins and bottles just disappeared as Kalo had.

Then Rohan turned and ran even faster. He ran into the big road that went round the mosque. Just in time he remembered that he might meet his father there, for he had a cycle repair shop at the foot of the mosque

steps. So he whirled around again. He kept going in circles, as if he were a little mad. At last he ran to the banyan tree, climbed over its roots into a cleft between two folds of the huge trunk and hid there, trembling.

'I'll hide this terrible rubber,' he said at last. 'I'll put it back in the hole and never, never take it out again.'

With shaking fingers he scraped more dust from the little hole he had dug earlier, in order to bury the rubber.

As he scraped and dug with trembling fingers, he found something else in the hole. At first he saw only one end of it – it was long and yellow. He dug harder and found it was a pencil. Quite a new pencil – he could see no one had used it before, though it looked old from being buried in the earth. He stopped crying and trembling as he wondered who could have buried a pencil here, and whether it was a magic pencil as the rubber was a magic one. He had to try it and see.

First he dropped the rubber into the hole and covered it up. Then he held up the pencil and pointed it at the bare patch of earth where the school had once stood between the warehouse and green-roofed house. Very, very carefully he drew a picture of his old white school building in the air. He did it so carefully that he seemed to see the grey lines forming before his eyes. Then he blinked: the grey-white building really *was* there now. Or was it only a picture in his mind? Quickly he drew the verandas, the playground, the high wall, and then the little matchstick figures of a line of schoolboys rushing out of the front gate, the lane filling with them, and saw them leaping and running with their satchels flying behind them.

He stood up and ran a little way down the lane, out of the shade of the mysteriously whispering banyan tree. Now, in the clear sunlight, he could see the school quite plainly again, alive and noisy with children set free from their lessons. He stood there till he saw the teacher come out on his bicycle. Then he turned and ran the other way up the lane.

He stood in the middle of the dusty road and quickly, quickly, drew a picture of a little black dog in the air, as well as he could. He was still working on the long plumed tail when he heard Kalo bark, and saw him bounce down on to the road on his four feet and come pelting towards him.

As he came closer, Rohan saw he had missed out the jagged edge of Kalo's ear where it had been torn in a dog-fight. He was careful to add that so Kalo would be exactly as he had been before, scarred and dusty and wild with happiness. Kalo stood still, waiting for him to finish.

When it was done, he shouted 'Kalo! Kalo!' and patted him hastily, then went on busily with his pencil, drawing the old, bearded tin-and-bottle man. He was just drawing the big, bulging sack when he heard the cracked voice cry '-o-ttle man!' and there he was, shuffling down the road and blinking a little in the bright light.

Then Rohan and his dog ran home, up the stairs to the empty roof-top. There, leaning against the low wall, his tongue between his teeth and his eyes narrowed, Rohan drew a picture of his home as well as he could. Even when he could see it quite plainly, the little whitewashed room with its arched windows and pigeon-roost on the flat roof, he went on drawing. He drew a picture of his mother kneading dough in a pan, the fire, the glass of milk and even the broom in the corner of the room. Then he went in and found them all there, just as he had drawn them. But he saw one mistake he had made in his drawing – he had coloured his mother's hair black and left out the grey strands over her ears. She had remained stiff, lifeless. He stood in the doorway, rubbing gently at the unnatural darkness of her hair till it showed the grey he knew. He realized you cannot draw a picture out of desperation, or with careless speed. It took care, attention, time.

When he had finished, his mother moved, looked up at him. 'There's your milk,' she said quietly, 'drink it up.'

He nodded. 'I'll sweep up a bit first,' he said, and went to fetch the broom. He swept and he swept, enjoying the work that he had not wanted to do at first, till he heard his father arrive, lean his bicycle against the wall and lock it, then come slowly up the stairs.

Rohan ran out, shouting, 'Look, I found a pencil and a rubber on the road today.' He wanted so much to tell his father all about it and ask him how it happened, but he did not dare.

His father was looking tired. 'Why don't you sit quietly and draw something?' he said, as he went in for his tea.

Rohan nodded and went to fetch a piece of paper. Then he sat on the top step and spread out the paper and drew. He was not sure if the magic pencil would draw an ordinary picture. It did. Using it very, very carefully now, he drew a picture of Kalo.

When his father saw it, he beamed. He had never seen a picture as good. Rohan showed it to his mother too, and she was so pleased she pinned it on the wall, next to the calendar.

His father said, 'I didn't know you could draw so well. Your teacher never told us. You should draw a picture for him.'

Rohan spent the whole evening drawing with the magic pencil. He took the drawings to school next day and his teacher was so pleased with them that he forgot to ask for an answer to his angry letter of the day before. He gave Rohan good paper and time to draw every day.

Rohan drew so much that the magic pencil was soon worn to a stub. Instead of throwing it away like an ordinary pencil, he took it down to the banyan tree and buried it in the earth at its roots where he had hidden the lump of rubber. As he walked away he worried about whether he would be able to draw as well with an ordinary pencil bought at the stationery shop near the school gate. But he had had so much practice now, and become so good an artist, that he found he could do as good a drawing with the new pencil he bought as with the magic one.

He became so famous in that town that people came from miles away to see the pictures his mother pinned to the walls of their house. They went to the school and asked the teacher about him. No one knew how he had learnt to draw and paint so well without any lessons or help. Even when he became a great artist, whose name was known all over the land, Rohan did not tell anyone the story. That was his secret – and the banyan tree's, and they kept it to themselves as secrets should be kept.

From *Guardian Angels*

What the children said:

'It was like a dream to me.'

'I wish I could rub out my school.'

Lutey and the Mermaid

Susan Price

In Curey, in Cornwall, there once lived a man named Lutey. He made his living, in the main, as a fisherman, although he grew vegetables in a small garden beside his cottage, and was not above robbing a wrecked ship, coming home with oranges and lemons in his shirt, or rolling a cask of doubly-salted butter along the beach, or carrying a small keg of wine on his shoulder. Sometimes, too, he would bring home a half-drowned passenger or ship's boy, for although quick to make a profit out of the disaster if he could, he was a kind man, who always gave what help he could to anyone in trouble.

One day, after a bad storm, Lutey was wandering along the beach, looking to see if the storm had washed up anything worth bending down to pick up, since the sea was still too rough for him to go fishing. His little mongrel dog was running in circles round him, coming back whenever he saw his master stop, to sniff at what had been found. Lutey picked up a couple of coins, and some bottles which he thought he would wash out and sell, and then, in a pool of sea-water formed by some rocks, he found a mermaid. He stood and looked at her for a long time, while his dog yapped from a safe distance. Lutey knew that she was a mermaid by the long, strong, coiling tail, all silver and blue, which formed her body from the waist down. Above the waist – well; she was more beautiful than the most beautiful woman Lutey had ever seen. His own wife had been pretty enough for anyone when he had married her, but even combed and washed, and dressed in her best, she had not looked like this creature. His wife's skin was brown and red; the mermaid's was white, absolutely white; as white as the full moon on a clear night.

His wife's eyes and hair were dark brown, like his own; the mermaid's hair was almost as white as her skin, but as the wind lifted first one strand and then another, green and blue and yellow lights flickered through it; and her eyes were large and grey. Over all the years Lutey's wife had grown stocky and almost shapeless with keeping house for him, and having his children; and although, when he had married her, Lutey had known this would happen, and although he loved her none the less for it, yet he was held by the sight of the mermaid's heart-breakingly slender arms and neck, and he shook his head in wonder and astonishment, and hoped that he would never forget one line or colour of the sight.

At last the mermaid, who had been staring at him and winding long strands of her hair round her fingers, stretched out her beautiful arms to him, and said, 'The storm washed me up here, lad; wouldst carry me back?'

Lutey started at the sound of her voice, but then grinned through his beard, and said, 'Aye; I reckon I could carry a little thing thing like thee down to the water, even if it is a mile out;' and he climbed into the pool, and lifted the mermaid in his arms. She put her arms about his neck, coiled her long tail round his waist, and laid her head against his shoulder. 'Parson wouldn't like this if he could see it,' Lutey said, 'but he can't, and I shan't tell him.' And he began to carry the mermaid over the long stretch of sand to the sea's edge. His little dog ran after him.

'Thou'rt a good man,' said the mermaid, and rubbed her cold cheek against his beard. 'If I could grant wishes, and I said I would give thee three, what wouldst wish for, lad?'

'That would take some thinking about,' Lutey said.

'Think, then, love,' said the mermaid.

'Well . . .' said Lutey. 'Well . . . there's a lot suffer from aches and pains, especially in this cold weather. I know my poor old gel does, and it catches me sharp sometimes, in the back, when I bend – and then there's fevers, and coughs and colds and all sorts. Aye; I reckon I'd wish for the power to heal if I was going to wish. That'd do some good for a lot of folk, that would.'

'And the second wish?'

'Well . . . folk lose a lot of things, and most of 'em bain't got that much that they can afford to lose it; so I'd wish next for the power to discover things lost. That'd be a help.'

'And the third wish, love?'

'Well . . . Those other wishes wouldn't be much help if they died with me, would they? Not that I'm old, but I'm getting on. So, I'd wish that the powers could pass down to my sons and daughters. Aye; that I would.'

He felt a coldness on his cheek as the mermaid kissed him. 'Thou'rt a good man,' she said. 'As good as thou'rt handsome.' And she kissed him three times more; on the eyelid, on the neck and on the lips.

'Hey, hey, hey,' Lutey said. 'Madam! I hope my old gel bain't looking this way. I got to go back to her, tha knowst.'

'Come with me instead,' said the mermaid, and clung to him more tightly. 'Come with me, love. You sail over the water in your boats, you men; hast never wondered what lies beneath it? Deep, deep beneath?'

'I have wondered,' said Lutey; 'but I should drown.'

'I wouldn't let thee drown, lad,' said the mermaid. 'I'd take thee where no man that breathes air has ever been; and I'd love thee.'

Lutey reached the edge of the sea, and, shaking his head, he waded into it, carrying the mermaid to where the water was deep enough for her to swim away. 'I can't come,' he said.

The mermaid tightened her arms and tail about him with frightening strength. 'Come with me, and be my love,' she said. 'Come with me and see the sunken ships with their sails all torn into rags and drifting with the tides; come and see what they were carrying, all spilt, all spoilt; come and search for coins in the sand down there, Lutey, my Handsome; come and dig for lost rings and broken necklaces; and for every precious stone you find, I'll give you another kiss.' And she kissed him again, with a touch even colder than before; a cold that struck him through, and yet was strangely pleasant, exciting, thrilling. And if he had wondered before what lay beneath the sea and its changing colours, now he wondered and longed to know, ten times more.

'Why stay here above the lovely water?' the mermaid asked, as she stroked his hair. 'Why suffer the storms and the pains; why work and worry, and run after every little thing that might put a crumb in your mouth? We don't live so under the sea: we never worry about what might happen; we never worry about food; we have no needs. Let go, my love; let go of your sorry world; come with me; sink with me into the darkness. Oh come with me, Lutey; come with me, love; be my love, Sweet; come with me.'

Lutey shivered as her cold kisses stole the strength from him, and he sank to his knees in the water. The sea rushed up against his chest and splashed about the mermaid. He opened his mouth, and was about to say that he would go with her, when, from the edge of the sea came the sound of his little dog barking. The mermaid, startled, loosened her hold, and Lutey looked round.

Beyond the noisy little dog he saw the beach he had walked along that morning; and beyond the beach he saw the small, poor cottage where he lived. He saw

smoke rising from holes in the roof; he saw his wife in
the vegetable garden, stooping to pull something up;
and he saw three of his children running, one after
another, on to the beach. He knew then that he could
not go with the mermaid, and he felt such sorrow at
that, and for the dwindling, wasted life of his wife, and
for the lives of his children which were yet to waste,
that he felt a pain as if a knife had been driven into him,

and tears came into his eyes. 'Oh, Sea-maid,' he said. 'I would come – I would come – but look, dost see my old gel back there? My poor old gel; if I go with thee, who's to dig the garden for her when her back aches, and get the vegetables in for next year? See the holes in the roof? Who'd mend 'em? See the smoke? Who'd chop the wood for the fire? Who'd find the money to feed and clothe the little uns if I wasn't here? No; my old gel she's too old now to do any better for herself than me, and I've got to stay and look after her.'

The mermaid wrapped her arms tightly round his neck, lashed out with her tail, and dragged him beneath the water. But Lutey was a strong man, and the water was not yet very deep. He struggled, and brought his head into the air again; and he dragged his knife from his belt and held it before the mermaid's face, knowing that all such creatures are afraid of cold iron; and he said, 'Go, in God's name!'

The water turned foamy and white all round him as the mermaid swam away; but at a distance she rose from the water again, and she called, 'Thou'rt a good man, Lutey, and each one of they three wishes shall be granted. I prophesy, too, that neither thee nor any of they children, nor thy children's children, nor any born of thy line shall ever, from this day, be hungry or cold. But thou art mine, Lutey, and I shall have thee. I grant thee nine more years to live in the air, and then I shall come and fetch thee home, lad.' Then she sank beneath the water, and Lutey waded back from the sea to his family.

Within a few days he had a chance to test the truth of the mermaid's words, for his youngest child fell sick, and could not sleep; but after Lutey had stroked her head and kissed her, she did sleep, and woke cured. It soon spread, from house to house, and village to village, that Lutey of Curey could heal, and people began to come to him when they were in pain, or feverish, or had wounds which had turned bad, or sores, or coughing-fits; and Lutey's skill and touch always brought ease. When it became known that he could also discover things that were lost, still more people came to him, and they all brought payment in eggs, or cake, or milk, or cheese, and sometimes in money, fulfilling the mermaid's prophecy that Lutey's children would never again be cold or hungry.

On the ninth anniversary of the day he had found the mermaid, Lutey went fishing, taking with him one of his youngest sons, a boy barely eight years old, who already possessed some of his father's powers. They fished all day, made a good catch, and, as the light was beginning to fade, and they were thinking of putting back to shore, the mermaid suddenly rose from the water near the boat, stretched out her lovely arms, and called Lutey's name.

Lutey immediately stood, and moved as though to jump overboard. His son, though very frightened, was quick enough to reach out and clutch at his father's legs. Lutey looked down at him impatiently. 'I stayed then,' he said. 'Now let me go.' The boy released him in bewilderment, and Lutey threw himself into the sea. He sank, and did not rise, for the mermaid dragged him down with her.

Lutey's son was left alone in the still rocking boat, the air growing cold and dark over the sea. He rowed home alone without his father, and no trace of Lutey was ever seen after that; neither his body, nor his clothes, nor anything belonging to him was ever washed up for mortals to find.

Lutey's son grew, and came into all the powers his father had had; and others of his own, for after he had seen the mermaid take his father, he always looked so hard for what was not to be seen that at last he saw its shadows – moving shadows at the edges and corners of rooms; shadows among trees and stone field-walls of the land, and among the rocks of the beach; shadows miming what was yet to happen.

But he never lived to have children, this second-sighted Lutey, for he still followed his father's trade of fisherman, and nine years after his father's disappearance, he went fishing with his younger brother; and the mermaid rose from the water and called to him. Without a word, without any hesitation, Young Lutey swung himself over the boat's side into her arms, and sank with her into the deep, cold sea.

His brother lived to marry, and his children inherited the family's gifts, as did their children, and indeed, for many generations there were no healers in Cornwall so famous as the Luteys of Curey; but every nine years the mermaid rose from the water and called for her payment; and another Lutey was drowned.

From *The Carpenter and Other Stories*

What the children said:

'It somehow made me believe it was true.'

'It made me want to cry when Lutey drowned.'

Film Boy

Alexander McCall Smith

Prem lived in Bombay. He had always lived there and he knew that Bombay was the most important city in all India. There was always so much going on – there were vast factories with smoking chimneys, shops and bazaars that seemed to go on and on for ever, and, most important of all, there were the film studios. Prem loved to go to the cinema. Sitting in his seat at the Regal Picture House, he would watch the exciting films that were made right there in Bombay.

The way Prem got the money for his cinema tickets was to work for it. Every day, after school, he would call in at the sweet stall which stood outside the nearby hospital. Mr Rahna, who owned the stall, did not have an assistant, and this made it hard for him to get away to have coffee with his friends. For half an hour or so each afternoon Prem would look after the stall for him, selling the sweetmeats to passers-by and putting the money in the cash box.

'Who do you think is the best film star?' a friend asked Prem one day.

Prem thought for a moment. 'Well,' he replied, 'Jani Sudha is very good. And I like Goel Prakash. But the very best, I think, is Rasi Pariwalar.'

Prem's friend looked thoughtful. 'I think you're right,' he said. 'I've heard people say he's the best in the world.'

'He is,' Prem said firmly. 'I'm sure he is.'

They had both seen many films starring Rasi and had enjoyed them all. Rasi was always the hero. If there was somebody who needed to be rescued, then Rasi would be the one to do it. It did not matter if the danger came from a flood or from a tiger, Rasi would not hesitate. Then, if the police were having difficulty in arresting a bandit, Rasi would be the person to whom they would turn. There was no limit to what he could do.

There was no mistaking Rasi. He was a tall man, with broad shoulders, and teeth that glinted like pinpoints of light when he smiled. His famous voice was deep – almost a growl when he was angry – but in the middle of a fight it could sound more like a shriek. That was a sound that would always send a shiver of fear down the spines of his enemies. Prem had often wondered what Rasi would look like in the flesh. Would he look so daring as he did on the screen? Would he look quite so impressive? Prem had no idea – that is, until the day he saw him.

This is how it happened. Prem had gone to Mr Rahna's stall at his usual time. Business was a bit quiet that day, Mr Rahna had said, and it would not have surprised Prem if he sold no sweetmeats at all. In fact, Prem might well have dozed off in the heat, had a large car not suddenly stopped in the street outside the stall and an unmistakeable figure stepped out. It was Rasi Paliwalar.

'Which of these sweets do you recommend?' the famous voice had asked.

'They're all very fresh, sir,' Prem said. His voice sounded shaky and he hoped that Rasi would not laugh.

'I'm sure they are,' Rasi replied pleasantly. 'But which taste best?'

Prem pointed out a tray of mango-flavoured fudge.

'Many people like that one, Mr Paliwalar.'

Rasi looked up. 'You go to the films?' he asked.

'Oh yes, sir,' Prem said. 'I go every week.'

Rasi nodded. 'Good,' he said simply. 'Now I'll take

ten pieces of that mango fudge.'

Prem took the coins which Rasi offered him and handed over the sweets. Rasi smiled again and then, without saying goodbye, dashed back across the road to the waiting car. The driver pulled out into the road, changed gear, and sped off.

Prem looked at the coins in his hand. Rasi had given him three times more than he needed to pay. Many people would have kept the extra money, but not Prem. It did not matter if Mr Paliwalar was rich – which he undoubtedly was. The extra money belonged to the film star, and Prem was determined that he would get it back. Besides, if he gave it back to him, Prem would have the chance to meet his hero again, and that was something he would like very much indeed.

Bombay is a great city. There are millions of people living there and to find one person out of all those millions is not simple. Eventually, though, Prem found out where Rasi lived and made his way to the wealthy street of great houses. His heart sank as he saw the gates of Rasi's mansion. They were twice as tall as he was and topped with menacing iron spikes. The garden wall, which ran along the edge of the road, was just as high and was also spiked. It was clear that the only way into the house was by invitation.

Prem walked up to the gates and peered shyly through the bars. Just inside the garden there was a small shed, from which an attendant immediately appeared.

'Go away,' he shouted, gesturing angrily. 'Get away from here.'

Prem drew back. 'I want to see Mr Paliwalar,' he

shouted out, trying not to seem too frightened of the guard's unwelcoming manner.

'You want to see Mr Paliwalar,' the guard sneered. 'The whole world wants to see Mr Paliwalar. You can go and see him in the cinema any day. Now run along!'

'But I've got to give him something,' Prem persisted. 'I must see him.'

The guard shook his head. 'Don't waste my time, little boy. Now are you going to go away or am I going to have to come out and beat you with my stick?'

Prem looked nervously at the stout pole that the guard was carrying. As keen as he was to see Rasi, he was not going to argue with that particular guard. No, ther must be a less risky way of getting through.

'All right,' he said. 'Don't worry. I'm going away.'

He did not go away, though. Just at the moment, a delivery truck arrived and sounded its horn. As the guard opened the gates to let the truck enter, Prem shot in on the other side. Nobody saw him do it, and nobody saw him creep up to the great house and on to its shady verandah. There was a large glass door that led off the verandah and into the house. As Prem peered in, he heard distant notes of music coming from deep within. There was certainly somebody at home – probably the film star himself.

Prem decided to knock on the glass door. It was not a loud knock and it was completely lost in the vast entrance hall that lay beyond. He knocked again, more firmly this time, but the sound still seemed too faint. Gently, he pushed open the door and stepped inside.

Prem looked about the entrance hall. It was a magnificently furnished room, hung with brightly coloured weavings and ivory trophies. A tiger's head with fixed, glaring eyes was mounted on one wall, and on another there was the stuffed head of an antelope.

Quietly he moved through the hall and into the room beyond. This was a living room, a room which stretched out in all directions. At one end there was a large piano topped with vases of flowers, at another end there were sofas and chairs covered with zebra skin. In the middle of the room there was a marble mosaic floor in the shape of a giant star, with each point a different colour.

Prem stood in silent wonderment. He had seen rooms like this in films, but he had never imagined that there would be such places right here in Bombay. He pictured the parties which must have taken place in this room – the swirl of colour from the pure silk saris, the laughter, the tinkling of ice in glasses, the music . . .

'Thief!' a voice rasped behind him. 'It's no good running. I've locked the door!'

The servant had entered the room so quietly that Prem had been quite unaware of his presence. The first thing he had felt was the tight grip on his arms and the sudden pain as they were forced behind his back. Then he heard the voice of his captor and the awful accusation.

Prem struggled to free himself, but this only made the servant push his arms higher. There was no point in resisting, he thought; I'm trapped.

'I'm not a thief,' he shouted out. 'I'm here to see Mr Paliwalar.'

'Don't lie to me!' the servant hissed. 'I know you thieving boys. We've caught you before.'

'I'm not lying,' Prem persisted. 'I knocked on the door. There was no reply.'

'Ah!' cried the servant, twisting Prem's arm. 'A thief who knocks on the door! A very polite thief!'

The pressure on Prem's arms suddenly slackened, although he was still tightly held. Prem felt himself being turned round and then frog-marched out of the room.

'Where are you taking me?' he asked. 'You must let me go.'

The servant laughed. 'Oh we'll let you go. Certainly we'll let you go. Once the police have arrived, we'll let you go then.'

They crossed the hall and went through a small door that led towards the back of the house.

'Please don't twist my arm,' Prem begged the servant. 'I won't run away now.'

The servant relaxed the pressure slightly and Prem made no move to escape. Sensing this, the servant's grip became even slacker. It was at this moment that Prem saw his chance. They had reached a point in the corridor where a staircase wound off on one side. It was the only possible escape that had presented itself so far and Prem took it. Wresting his arms free, he hurled himself away from the servant, pushing him over as he did so. There was a shout and a crash as the servant stumbled and Prem leapt up the stairs.

'Thief!' shouted the enraged voice below him. 'Thief!'

Prem mounted the stairs three at a time. Reaching the top, he saw that he was in another corridor. There were no windows, he noticed, and so he decided to run headlong wherever the corridor took him. There were two doors at the end, one of them ajar, the other closed. Prem pushed open the door which was slightly ajar and then slammed it shut behind him. Turning round, he bent over to recover his breath. When he looked up, he saw that there was a man sitting writing at a desk near the window.

Rasi Paliwalar spun round in astonishment. From down the corridor there came the sound of running feet and the voice of the angry servant.

'Mr Paliwalar! Mr Paliwalar! There's a thief loose in the house!'

Rasi laid down his pen and stared hard at Prem.

'So,' he said coldly. 'So we have a thief.'

Prem stood where he was, unable to move, unable to speak. Behind him the door opened sharply and the servant burst in breathlessly.

'Here he is, Mr Paliwalar. I have caught him now.'

Prem felt the man's grip again and winced in pain. His arms were forced up behind his back, almost lifting him off his feet.

'No!' he shouted. 'I'm not a thief! I'm not!'

As Prem screamed out, Rasi rose from his desk.

'Let him go,' he said to the servant. 'You don't have to half kill him.'

The servant released his grip reluctantly and Prem felt the blood surge back into his arms. Rasi was looking at him curiously and he realised that this was his opportunity to explain.

'I'm not a thief, Mr Paliwalar,' Prem blurted out. 'I came to see you. You remember me.'

Rasi raised an eyebrow. 'Remember you? I don't know you, do I?'

Prem lowered his eyes. 'You came to our sweetmeat stall a few days ago. Near the hospital. I served you.'

Rasi was silent. 'Maybe,' he said. 'Maybe I did.'

'He's lying, sir,' the servant interrupted. 'These boys

lie and lie again. You mustn't believe him.'

'Quiet!' Rasi snapped. 'Let him have his say.'

Slowly, and stumbling over parts of the story, Prem told Rasi why he had wanted to see him. As he spoke, he thought how far-fetched the story sounded – if he had been in Rasi's place, would he believe that somebody would go to all that trouble just to return a few coins?

Suddenly the servant interrupted.

'If this is true, Mr Paliwalar,' he said. 'Then let him show us this money. That will prove it.'

Rasi looked at Prem inquisitively. 'Well?' he said. 'Why don't you show us this famous money?'

Prem smiled. 'Of course.' Then, dipping into his trouser pocket he felt for the familiar coins. For a moment his heart stopped. There was nothing there.

'Well?' urged Rasi. 'Let's see the money.'

Prum struggled to utter his reply. It was the end of his world now; nobody would believe him – he would be labelled a thief.

'I've lost it, Mr Paliwalar. I had it in my pocket, but it must have fallen out in the garden. I promise you it was there. I promise you . . . ' He tailed off, his voice becoming weaker.

'Ha!' shouted the servant. 'You see, Mr Paliwalar! I was right!'

Rasi looked at Prem and shook his head.

'It doesn't look good for you, does it?' he said quietly.

'No,' said Prem. 'But I promise you Mr Paliwalar, I'm not a thief.'

Rasi was quiet for a moment. Then he looked at the servant and issued an instruction.

'Take this young man outside,' he said. 'Let him

show you where he was in the garden. If he doesn't find the money, then you can call the police. If he finds it, then call me. Do you understand?'

The servant nodded. Holding firmly on to Prem's wrist, he led him out of the room and down the corridor.

The servant standing over him, Prem searched through the garden for the missing money. There was no sign of it, and soon the servant dragged him back into the house. There is one last chance, thought Prem: the stairs. The money might well have fallen there when he had made his dash up the stairs.

The servant tried to prevent him, but Prem managed to drag himself to the foot of the staircase. This was where he had launched himself away and this is where he had gone down on his hands and knees. It was exactly the sort of place where something might have fallen out of his pocket.

And that is just what had happened. There, on the third stair from the bottom, the coins lay where they had fallen, three small circles of metal, but in Prem's eyes the most welcome sight imaginable.

'I've found them!' Prem shouted. 'See! I told you that I had them!'

The servant looked at the coins suspiciously. 'Maybe they were dropped by somebody else,' he said. 'People are always coming and going on these stairs.'

'They're mine!' Prem protested. 'It's exactly the amount I told Mr Paliwalar I had. There, count them!'

He handed the coins to the servant, who looked at them doubtfully.

'No,' said the servant. 'These are not your coins. I myself lost some money on these stairs. These coins are mine.'

And with that, he slipped the coins into his pocket and reached out to grap Prem's arm.

'You're coming with me to the kitchen,' he said. 'We'll wait there for the police.'

'Let me go!' Prem shouted. 'I've found the money. Mr Paliwalar said you were to take me to him! Let me go!'

Prem fought against the servant's grasp but he was unable to free himself. He kicked at the man's shins, but missed, and was only rewarded with a hard blow to his chest. It's no use, he said to himself – there's nothing I can do.

And then he saw Mr Paliwalar standing above him on the stairs.

'Mr Paliwalar,' he shouted, 'I . . .'

Rasi raised a hand to silence him.

'I heard all that,' he said, his eyes fixed on the servant. 'You can let this young man go. I'll speak to you later.'

The servant dropped Prem's arm and shuffled off down the corridor. Prem looked back up at Rasi and noticed that he was smiling.

'I'm sorry I didn't believe you,' Rasi said, as he came down the stairs to where Prem was standing. 'I hope you'll let me make it up to you. I think that I owe you rather more than an apology. Don't you?'

Prem said nothing. Then Mr Paliwalar went on:

'How about a visit to the studio? he said. 'You'd like that, wouldn't you? What about next week?'

The following Friday, Rasi's car arrived at the promised time and Prem climbed in beside the driver. Half an hour later they were at the studio gate, a large, impressive set of pillars with the name of the film company written in gold letters over the top. The guard at the gate waved Rasi's car through and the driver nosed slowly into a parking place near a large building.

'Mr Paliwalar will meet you in his dressing room,' he said. 'If you go over to that booth they'll show you where to go.'

The dressing room had Rasi's name written on it. Prem bent down to dust his shoes and then, as confidently as he could, he knocked on the door. After a moment, the door was flung open by an assistant, who looked at Prem with irritation. He was about to tell Prem to go away when, from within the room, there came a shout.

'If that's my friend Prem,' Rasi called out, 'then show him in.'

As Prem entered the room, Rasi rose to his feet. He looked splendid. On his head he had a brilliant red turban, with flowing sash, and at his side he wore a wicked-looking curved sword.

'I'm playing a lancer today,' he explained, gesturing at the uniform. 'Come. Let's see what my director wants me to do.'

Prem and Rasi made their way through the echoing studios. All about, there were signs of feverish activity. Lights hung suspended from beams, camera tracks criss-crossed the floor and people rushed about with props and costumes. In one corner of the studio, a set had been made up to look like the deck of a boat, and two actors were busy heaving on ropes under the glare of the lights. In another part, a large black car was being edged into position in front of a garage set and several actors dressed as policemen were standing by, ready for filming.

'We're filming outside,' Rasi explained, as they left the main studio building. 'I think I'm meant to be rescuing somebody from a fortress. It'll be hot work!'

When they reached the mock-up of the fortress, Prem stood to one side as Rasi discussed his role with the director and his assistants. Then, when the other actors were in place, a man with a striped clapperboard stood in front of the cameras and brought the clapper down with a sharp snap. Rasi, who had mounted a horse, now rode up to the fortress in a cloud of dust. The most exciting two hours of Prem's life had just begun.

Several months later, Rasi's new film was released. Prem saw the posters advertising it go up outside the Regal Picture House and his heart swelled with pride at the thought that he had seen the filming.

The day before the film was due to be shown for the first time, Prem went to work as usual at the sweetmeat stand. Mr Rahna, who was expecting him, gave him a broad smile.

'Well, well,' he said genially. 'So there you are!'

'I hope I'm not late,' Prem said, glancing at the watch on Mr Rahna's wrist.

'Oh, you're not late,' Mr Rahna reassured him. 'It's just that somebody called to see you. A friend of yours.'

Prem was puzzled. He could not imagine who might come to see him at the stall, or at least who would bother Mr Rahna on his account.

'Yes,' went on Mr Rahna. 'A very well known friend . . .'

Prem caught his breath. Could it be? Dared he hope?

'Here,' said Mr Rahna. 'He left this for you.'

Prem took the envelope from Mr Rahna's hand and examined it carefully

'Go on,' urged Mr Rahna. 'Open it!'

Prem eased open the envelope flap. Inside was a letter with another piece of paper attached to it. He glanced quickly at the bottom of the page to see the signature:

Rasi Paliwalar.

'You see!' crowed Mr Rahna. 'Mr Paliwalar himself came round with that! With my own eyes I saw him! I shook his hand!' He paused. 'And what does he say? Come on!'

Prem read the letter and smiled.

'It's two free tickets for the first Bombay showing of his new film,' he said. 'He also says he might see me again one day if he's passing this way.'

'Oh my!' exclaimed Mr Rahna. 'Two free tickets to the premiere! Who'll go with you?'

Prem paused and thought for a moment. There was really no doubt in his mind as to whom he should invite.

'You,' he said simply, and then: 'That is, if you'd like to go.'

'Would I like to go!' shouted Mr Rahna. 'Of course I'd like to go!'

As he spoke, Mr Rahna emerged from behind the counter and shook Prem by the hand.

'Oh my goodness!' he said, his voice becoming high with excitement. 'What an exciting occasion that will be!'

'Yes,' said Prem. 'It will.'

And that is just what it turned out to be. As Prem sat

in the darkness of the cinema, Mr Rahna at his side, he watched with pride as the great rescue scene came up on the screen. 'One day,' he muttered to himself, 'I'm going to work in that film studio.'

'Did you say something?' Mr Rahna asked.

Prem shook his head. Some plans, like some secrets, are best kept to ourselves.

What the children said:

'I believe that what happened in this story could happen in real life.'

'I could see in my head the pictures which were being described.'

Notes about the Authors

Aiken, Joan has written over fifty novels for children, one of which, THE WOLVES OF WILLOUGHBY CHASE, has been made into a full length feature film. Her children's writing falls into three categories – collections of short fairy tales, fantastic, supernatural, though often set in the present-day – full length novels for an older age group set in an imaginary nineteenth century – and stories for younger children about extra-intelligent talking animals.
Also by this author
A NECKLACE OF RAINDROPS and Other Stories (Cape)
THE LAST SLICE OF RAINBOW and Other Stories (Cape)

Appiah, Peggy has been a collector of folk tales over many years, but started collecting seriously when, on her marriage, she went to live in Ghana. She confesses to being totally amazed by the sense of humour and inventiveness of these stories, which are still so much part of Ghanaian life.
Also by this author
THE PINEAPPLE CHILD and Other Tales from Ashanti (Deutsch)

Beckley, Ruth was a contributor to E. J. Arnold's FOLK TALES OF THE WORLD series in the 1960s. She was widely-travelled, and WAMBU THE DUCK was part of a series of unusual animal myths from Australia.

Cameron, Ann is a writer from the United States, whose books about Julian's lively black family have become favourites here. They were inspired by the childhood memories of a friend. Julian and his brothers continue their adventures in MORE STORIES JULIAN TELLS and JULIAN'S GLORIOUS SUMMER (Gollancz)

Desai, Anita is one of India's best contemporary writers and lives in Bombay. She writes deeply and sympathetically

about her characters in stories that are evocative of the atmosphere and landscape of India. SECRETS appeared in a collection of stories by Guardian Children's Fiction Award winners.
Also by this author
THE PEACOCK GARDEN (Heinemann)
THE VILLAGE BY THE SEA (Heinemann)

Goble, Paul was born in England, but has had a lifelong interest in the lives of the Plains Indians. He has written and illustrated nine books about them. Many are re-creations of North American Indian legends, and he uses traditional native art as the inspiration for his paintings. THE GIRL WHO LOVED WILD HORSES won the Caldecott Medal in America. The author regards his stories and paintings as gifts to the Native People, who have for many years had their heritage withheld from them. 'All I am doing is to give back to the people the things that are really theirs,' he says. He now lives in the Black Hills of Dakota.
Also by this author
STAR BOY (Collier Macmillan)
HER SEVEN BROTHERS (Collier Macmillan)

Greaves, Margaret is an author who writes for a wide age group, and is also an anthologist. She is a countrywoman, and has a particular feeling for natural things, an interest in the past, and a leaning towards folklore and magic. Above all, she is interested in people and human relationships, and her books reflect this strongly.
Also by this author
CHARLIE, EMMA AND THE DRAGON stories (Methuen)
LITTLE BEAR AND THE PAPAGINI CIRCUS (Methuen)
HETTY PEGLER, HALF WITCH·(Methuen)

Hallworth, Grace grew up in the West Indies. When she was a child there was nothing she liked better than to listen and to read stories, especially those which are part of the islands' customs, folklore and humour. The retellings are full of vitality and expression and have the right amount of humour to captivate children from a very early age.

Also by this author
MOUTH OPEN, STORY JUMP OUT (Methuen)
CARNIVAL KITE (Methuen)

Hamilton, Virginia is one of the most distinguished writers for children today. M. C. HIGGINS THE GREAT was awarded more honours in the year of its publication than any other children's book. Her book of American Black folktales is based on a lifetime of study and interest. She received an award for the best juvenile mystery for her book THE HOUSE OF DIES DREAR.

Also by this author
SWEET WHISPERS, BROTHER RUSH (Walker Books)
LITTLE LOVE (Gollancz)

Hedlund, Irene is a Danish writer whose story from Japan was translated by Judith Elkin, who has a particular interest in the multi-ethnic origins of children's stories.

McCall Smith, Alexander was born in Zimbabwe and was educated both there and in Scotland. He is Senior Lecturer in law at the University of Edinburgh, and has worked in Africa and in the United States. He writes for both children and adults, and one of his most recent adult publications was CHILDREN OF WAX, a collection of African folktales set in Matabeleland.

Also by this author (for children)
THE WHITE HIPPO (Hamish Hamilton)
THE PERFECT HAMBURGER (Hamish Hamilton)
MIKE'S MAGIC SEEDS (Corgi)

O'Brien, Edna was born in the West of Ireland, and is the celebrated author of over ten adult novels, three plays and five collections of short stories. She was the winner of the 1971 Yorkshire Post Novel Award, and now lives in London with her two sons.

Also by this author (for children)
THE DAZZLE (Hodder and Stoughton)
A CHRISTMAS TREAT (Hodder and Stoughton)

Price, Susan is an author who has the ability to get inside her characters, making her stories real and immediate, funny and touching. She has written both historical and contemporary novels, but her more recent fiction has tended towards ghost stories and other fantasies. In these tales Susan Price's down-to-earth style makes the reader believe utterly in the supernatural atmosphere she has created. She won the Carnegie Medal in 1988 for THE GHOST DRUM.
Also by this author
HERE LIES PRICE (Faber)
THE BONE DOG (Scholastic)
CRACK-A-STORY (Faber)

Proysen, Alf was a Norwegian writer, born in 1914. His Mrs Pepperpot stories were an immediate success when first published and have been translated into several languages. Alf Proysen also wrote many other stories and poems for children, as well as a weekly newspaper column. He died in 1971.
Also by this author
LITTLE OLD MRS PEPPERPOT (Hutchinson)
MRS PEPPERPOT'S BUSY DAY (Hutchinson)
MRS PEPPERPOT'S CHRISTMAS (Hutchinson)

Williams-Ellis, Amabel was born in 1894 into a literary family. She wrote novels and non-fiction, but is perhaps best-known as a reteller of traditional folk and fairy tales from all over the world. She was married to the famous architect, Sir Clough Williams-Ellis, and died in 1984.
Also by this author
ROUND THE WORLD FAIRY TALES
OLD WORLD FAIRY TALES
NEW WORLD FAIRY TALES

Acknowledgements

The editors would like to thank the following authors and publishers in granting permission for their stories to be used in this collection, to benefit the Federation of Children's Book Groups Project, Story Aid:

Octopus Children's Publishing for 'Once There Were No Pandas' by Margaret Greaves, and 'Quaka Raja' by Grace Hallworth from *Listen to this Story*, both published by Methuen Children's Books; A. & C. Black Ltd for 'Mighty Mountain and the Three Strong Women' by Irene Hedlund; Hodder and Stoughton Children's Books for 'The Great White Cat' from *The Enchanted World* by Amabel Williams-Ellis; A. M. Heath & Co. Ltd for 'Baba Yaga's Daughter' from *The Kingdom Under the Sea* by Joan Aiken, published by Jonathan Cape Ltd; A. P. Watt Ltd and Victor Gollancz Ltd for 'The Pudding Like a Night on the Sea' from *The Julian Stories* by Ann Cameron; Macmillan Children's Books for 'The Girl Who Loved Wild Horses' by Paul Goble; David Higham Associates Ltd for 'How Kwaku Ananse was Punished for his Bad Manners' from *Tales of an Ashanti Father* by Peggy Appiah, published by Andre Deutsch Ltd; Century Hutchinson Ltd for 'The Ski-Race' from *Mrs Pepperpot to the Rescue* by Alf Proysen; Duncan Heath Management for 'Two Giants' from *Tales for the Telling* by Edna O'Brien, published by Pavilion Books; The Estate of the Late A. W. Crown for 'Wambu the Duck' from *Folk Tales of the World* published by E. J. Arnold; Alfred A. Knopf Inc., New York, for 'The People Could Fly' from *American Black Folk Tales* by Virginia Hamilton, published by Walker Books; Anita Desai for her story 'Secrets' from *Guardian Angels*, published by Viking Kestrel; Faber and Faber Ltd for 'Lutey and the Mermaid' from *The Carpenter and Other Stories* by Susan Price; Alexander McCall Smith for 'Film Boy', adapted by the author from a story first published by Methuen Children's Books.

We would also like to thank St James Press for biographical information obtained from their publication *Twentieth Century Children's Writers*.

Finally our thanks to all the testers, co-ordinators, and the children who have worked hard to make this collection possible.